HAVING IT ALL

THE PUNISHMENT PIT ~ BOOK THREE

LIVIA GRANT

Published by Black Collar Press

Having it All
Punishment Pit Series - Book Three
by Livia Grant

e-book ISBN: **978-1-947559-36-3**
Print ISBN: **978-1-947559-37-0**

Cover Art by Laura Hidalgo and Spellbinding Creations

First Electronic Publish Date, September 2020

First Print Publish Date, September 2020

**Submission is an addiction she thought
she'd left behind,
but who can say no to him?**

Best friends are always supposed to be there for
each other,
but walking into a place like The Punishment Pit
was above and beyond.

Now Master Lukus is holding her captive,
intent on punishing Tiffany for her mistakes,
and instead of saving Brianna,
she's trapped with a man from her darkest fantasies.

She's in way over her head. Falling too hard, too
fast.
And the dangerously dominant owner of the club is
pushing all her buttons,
waking up every naughty desire she'd ever had and
more.

CHAPTER ONE

MARKUS

The room was dark, illuminated by only a few dying votive candles about to be snuffed out like the dozen others had been before them. Markus contemplated getting up to blow the last candles out but didn't want to disturb his sleeping wife tucked against his body.

Brianna was nearly sleeping on top of him, her right arm and leg thrown over his naked body, her head tucked under his arm as she snuggled close, using his chest as her pillow. He smiled down at his wife. Even in sleep, it seemed she wanted to stay as physically close to him as possible. He knew just how she felt.

Hell, I'd sleep buried inside of her if my dick would cooperate.

After their wild ride on the stage downstairs, and another quickie once upstairs, Brianna had somehow managed to fall into a deep sleep once they got to Lukus's guest room. Considering she'd had little-to-no sleep the night before—coupled with the emotional and physical upheaval of her last twenty-four hours of punishment—her exhaustion made sense.

As drained as he was, Markus found himself staying awake just to listen to the comforting sounds of his wife's slow and steady breathing. The mishmash of visions floating through his brain made sleep impossible for the recently revived Dom.

Damn, she was beautiful tonight on stage, the perfect vision of submission with her gorgeous body responding to the pain, allowing it to bring her pleasure. I was sure Lukus had been full of shit.

Feelings of sexual dominance he'd long ago learned to suppress were now coursing through his body. Markus was giving those feelings free rein after having kept them locked away from the mistaken fear of scaring Brianna. How wrong he'd been. If only he had known of his wife's deep need to submit—a need that drove her to the arms of a former lover. Now, in the fallout of Brianna's infidelity, the lockbox where he'd kept his feelings hidden away had sprung open. Memories and emotions he'd thought long gone had resurfaced with a vengeance.

If the reawakening of his dominant nature were

the only thing weighing on the recycled-Dom, he might have been able to find some peace. Unfortunately, his dominant tendencies were not the only memories he'd locked away. Markus had also managed to stuff the regret over how he'd failed his ex-wife Georgie at the end of their marriage into that same small box. Now the guilt spilling out was threatening to drown him.

It felt wrong to be thinking of his ex-wife while lying with the love of his life wrapped in his arms, but Markus knew if he was going to take his place as the Dom of his marriage, he had no choice but to deal with his failures from the past head-on to ensure he never made the same mistakes with Bri. He wallowed in his guilt for several long minutes more before regaining control of his wayward emotions.

Looking back, he'd known, even on the day they got married, he'd not given his whole heart to Georgie. Not really. At least, not in a way a husband should. He'd loved the idea of being married, and he had certainly loved dominating his beautiful full-time submissive, but even at the time he'd subconsciously known he used his natural dominance as a shield to keep not only his wife, but other aspects of his life, at arm's length. While that shield helped make him a successful lawyer, it made him a shitty husband.

Meeting Brianna had changed everything, and

Markus had promptly cut Lukus out of his life after meeting her. He'd told himself at the time he was just protecting Bri from being around the BDSM scene since it was through BDSM she'd met her former abusive boyfriend, Jake. But the raw truth was that Markus hadn't just cooled his friendship with Lukus because of Bri. It had just as much to do with his shame over how he'd let Lukus down when things fell apart with Georgie.

As hard as it was for Markus to admit, he'd been a coward. Lukus had been riding his ass for months after Georgie left and it was easier to cut Lukus out than it was to admit his own failings. Right or wrong, Markus had looked at Brianna as his do-over and he hadn't wanted any of his past mistakes to bleed over into his new marriage.

The fact Lukus had forgiven him was nothing short of a miracle. Markus made a silent pledge to never again let his invisible wall hold back his relationship with the closest thing he'd ever have to a brother.

Markus continued to let the memories of that failed night replay over and over until he felt almost sick to his stomach, unshed tears blurring his vision.

"Honey, what's wrong? Oh, my God, Markus. I'm so sorry I hurt you so much. Please, don't cry."

Markus had been so lost in his guilt as he remembered the second worst night of his life—last night being the worst—that he'd missed Brianna stirring awake by his barely suppressed sobs. To his utter shame, Markus found himself giving into his tears in front of his wife.

Way to go, Lambert. You find out your wife, the love of your life, is desperate for a strong Dom in her life and you can't stop yourself from crying every fucking ten minutes. Keep it up. You're going to lose her just like you lost Georgie. Fuck, maybe I don't deserve her anyway.

"Markus, please. Tell me what's wrong. You're scaring me." Brianna had raised herself up to look down at her husband from above. She used her fingers to brush at his tears. Her touch was soft and comforting.

There was just enough light left in the room from the remaining candles for Markus to see how concerned she was, and he wondered what he'd done to deserve a second chance at love with this beautiful, sexy woman. It was, in part, his inability to recognize her deep submissive needs that had driven her into the arms of another man. Now that he had her back, he wouldn't lose her again.

Swiping at his tears, he finally found his voice. "Bri, sweetheart. There's something I need to tell you."

An expression of mixed surprise and fear crossed her face. "Is everything okay, honey? Oh please, don't tell me you can't forgive me after all. I swear to you, I will never, *ever,* cheat on you again. I love you so much. I'll do any…"

Markus quieted his wife by placing two fingers

against her trembling lips. "Shush. I know you won't, sweetheart. It's not about that."

Brianna sighed. "What is it, Markus? What could have you so upset if it isn't what I did?"

Markus pushed into a sitting position, throwing a pillow behind his back as he leaned against the slated headboard.

Leave it to Lukus to have the perfect bed for tying down wayward subs.

He pulled Brianna to him, depositing her in his lap, their faces just inches apart. He wrapped his arms around her protectively, subconsciously cradling her as if to avoid letting her slip through his fingers again. He was nervous as hell, but as close as they were, they'd both been keeping way too many painful secrets from each other—secrets that had just about ruined their marriage. As afraid as he was to tell her everything, he knew he had no alternative. There would never again be any secrets between them. Not if he had anything to say about it.

Reaching to stroke her cheek, Markus took control. "Bri, it's clear we've both been keeping way too many things from each other and that's going to stop, starting tonight. It may take time, but we're gonna talk until we have nothing hidden, do you hear me? You're going to tell me more about what made you go to the BDSM clubs in the first place years ago and what it is you've been missing in our marriage that made you risk going anywhere with that asshole who hurt you so badly in the past."

When Brianna opened her mouth to speak, Markus gently moved his fingers to her lips again. "Not yet, baby. You're not the only one who's been keeping secrets. I need to go first. I need to tell you why I never told you about my being a Dom, about being a member of The Punishment Pit, and about why I never told you Georgie was my full-time submissive."

The surprise on her face made Markus smile. "Lukus told me you were a Dom and Rachel told me she's known you for years because you used to come to the club, but it feels different hearing you say it. Part of me worried they were making it up."

"A small part of me wishes they were, but they weren't. From my time experimenting in college until the day I met you, I considered myself a full-fledged, card-carrying Dom. Before I met you, I never considered being in a relationship that didn't include the BDSM lifestyle."

"So, what changed when you met me?" she softly asked.

"Brianna, there's a part of me that wishes I could have met you in one of the BDSM clubs before you met that asshole. I hate that you spent years of your life being brutalized by him, all the time thinking that was the way you were supposed to be treated... but..." Markus had to take a break to get the courage to continue. "But, in truth, I'm glad I didn't meet you then, because I might have turned out to be the one to hurt you instead of him."

Brianna gasped. The shock on her face cut him to the core. "I can't believe you would say that to me, Markus. You've never hurt me. Well, not before tonight, anyway."

"That's the hard part for me to admit to you, sweetheart," Markus explained. "I changed when I met you, and the reason I was able to change was because I fell in love with you the first night we met." He paused, his eyes locked onto hers. "But there's another darker reason—one I never admitted to anyone, not even to myself. Not until everything blew up yesterday and I finally thought things through. Do you remember the night we sat out on the balcony at the hotel in South Beach watching the ships, talking for hours?"

Her gorgeous smile returned to his lovely wife's face. "How could I ever forget that night, Markus? It was our first trip away together. We had only been dating a couple months, but I already knew I wanted to spend the rest of my life with you. I was so happy when you surprised me and whisked me away to Miami for the romantic getaway. Not only did we learn so much about each other but..." She blushed. "... it was our first time making love that night. I still can't believe you waited for me as long as you did, making sure I was ready after all Jake had done to me."

"It was one of the most important nights of my life, Bri, and I'd planned on telling you about me being a Dom that night, and about how I belonged to The Punishment Pit and how I had hopes of helping you put your fear behind you. But after you told me the details of the horrendous things he'd done and how afraid you were... you were so vulnerable. I could hear it in your voice. You were terrified of being hurt like that again. You associated all of the pain with the lifestyle, so I pledged that night to never again let anyone hurt you like that, not even me."

Her answer was only a whisper. "I wish you'd told me anyway, Markus."

"Maybe. Maybe not."

"How can you say that?"

"Because, in all truth, before I met you, I wasn't much different from Jake. I was a terrible Dom to Georgie, and that night as I listened to you talk about how his actions had impacted you, it made me understand that what I'd done to Georgie at the end of our marriage wasn't really much different than what Jake had done to you. It scared the shit out of me. I actually got sick to my stomach when I realized Georgie could be sitting somewhere at that very moment saying the exact same things about me, and she would have had every right. Do you remember how I got up and rushed to the bathroom at one point?"

"Yes." It was a whisper.

"I barely made it to the bathroom before I threw up from my disgust at myself."

Brianna had a look of incredulous disbelief on her face. "I don't... no, I *won't* believe it, Markus. There is nothing you can say to me that would make me believe you are even one percent like Jake. Nothing. Do you hear me?" She sounded so strong, her loyalty unwavering.

Damn, I don't know what I did to deserve this woman.

"You say that now, Bri. But you don't know what happened... what I did."

"So, tell me."

"It was a million little things... and one... fucking... terrible... unforgivable thing." When Brianna held silent, waiting expectantly, he finally plunged forward. "The last night... the night she'd finally had enough of my near-constant absence and got the courage to leave me... I hurt her. I let my anger take over and I tried to punish her into staying. I broke the most important rule of being a Dom. I didn't take care of her or protect her. I hurt her verbally, and when that didn't work, I hurt her physically. I even—fuck—I can't believe I have to say these words to you. I even blew through her safeword and continued to whip her with a bullwhip until Lukus had to tackle me to make me stop."

He heard the sharp intake of Brianna's breath and saw the flicker of shock cross her face before she quickly recovered. Markus waited, expecting to hear the disgust in her voice for what he had done. He wasn't prepared for her anger as she confronted him.

"Okay, so let's get a few things straight here, Markus. I'm going to ask you questions and I want you to tell me the truth, do you hear me?"

Markus couldn't help but crack a smile. She actually sounded like a bossy Domme right that minute.

"Yes, ma'am." His response brought a small smile to her lips.

"Okay, question number one. Did you allow Georgie to *have* a safeword before that night?"

"Of course."

"Okay, difference number one with Jake. I never got to even have a safeword until the very end. Next question. Before that night, had she ever needed to use her safeword?"

"Hell, no."

"Difference number two with Jake. I begged for him to stop so many times. That last weekend I must have screamed my new safeword ten times and not only did he not stop, but he actually laughed at me. Did you ever laugh at Georgie that night, Markus?" Before he could answer, she continued. "In fact, did you ever laugh at Georgie when you disciplined her or punished her?"

"Of course not, but...." It was Bri's turn to hold her fingers up to his lips to shush him.

She was on a roll. The next set of questions come so fast he had no time to answer. "Did you ever purposely humiliate her? Tie her down and punish her for hours on end while she begged you to stop? Did you ever cane her until you drew blood to satisfy your own sadism? Did you ever once fuck her so hard she was in pain for *weeks* after? Not hours. Not days, but fucking *weeks* because you had torn her?"

Brianna was shaking in his arms and he knew it wasn't just from the fearful memories, but from her anger. It had the desired effect of capturing his full attention. "Bri, sweetheart. You don't understand. I wasn't a very good husband or Dom to her and when I could see you were so afraid, it was almost a relief for me to be able to just turn my back on the D/s lifestyle. It's like I got a do-over. I didn't have to keep going back to the club and hear the whispers behind my back as I'd walk by. I didn't have to keep having my failures thrown up in my face. I got a fresh start and I've been truly happy. I want you to know that. I've never once regretted walking away. Well, not until I realized I'd failed you too by not picking up on your submissive needs."

Brianna's face was softening. Her brief bout of anger was subsiding. "Honey, that's my fault. I should have been more direct and talked to you about it. But I was embarrassed. I didn't think you would understand after all I'd told you about my relationship with Jake. I mean, you've been so gentle and loving with me and most of the time, that's exactly what I needed, even what I wanted. Without knowing you'd been a Dom and had lived the lifestyle before, how could I think for a minute you might understand my need to be dominated by you sometimes? Spanked and punished by you when I do something wrong? Tied down and taken hard when I least expect it just to show me I belong to you?"

Markus's heart was racing at her words. The mere thought of being able to spank Brianna's beautiful ass had his blood rushing to his cock. "You're right, sweetheart. I wish I'd told you while we were in Miami that weekend. At least then you'd have known you could have talked to me about your feelings if you ever felt the need to explore your submissiveness again. Still, after all the time we spend talking, it blows my mind you could hide your submissive feelings from me."

It was Brianna's turn to look guilty. "I know I should've found a way to talk to you. And you have to believe me—I truly didn't plan to cheat on you. Jake has always been good at figuring out my weaknesses and then going in for the kill. Yesterday, when he showed up, I had no intention of leaving with him, but he started by blackmailing me with things from my past and then...well, he just knows how to get under my skin. Then Tiffany got angry with me for not calling the police and we had a terrible fight over it and well... I just got mad and left with him. I knew as soon as I was in the car I was just running away because my best friend had made me feel so guilty. If I could go back and never leave with him, you have to believe me, I would. I'm so very sorry."

Markus had heard her apology a dozen times before and he'd already forgiven her. But that forgiveness hadn't completely cleansed him of the anger and hurt of knowing Brianna had given herself to another man.

"The fact you cheated on me—that you actually let someone else stick his dick in you—it cuts me to the core, Bri," he said. "It would have been bad enough if it had been some stranger. But the fact that it was the asshole who hurt you so bad —who laughed at your pain and humiliated you—I don't even know how to process this. I truly don't. You're so smart.... so strong... and then you do something so fucking stupid and dangerous!"

He paused, giving Brianna time for the impact of his words to sink in. "He could have killed you, Bri. I heard it in his voice. He's obsessed with you. He wants you back and he's just the kind of sick bastard who could decide if he can't have you then no one can. Did you ever once think about that?"

He felt his wife shaking in his arms. He hated that he'd scared her, but he knew he needed to say the words and she needed to hear them. If they were ever going to put her infidelity behind them, they had to acknowledge the unpleasant truths.

"You're right, Markus." Brianna wiped away a tear. "I spent most of last night in that cage lying awake thinking about it and I don't have any good reason other than temporary insanity. I don't know how you're ever going to forgive me, but I promise you, I'll do anything to earn your trust again."

Markus looked at his wife's beautiful tear-streaked face and decided it was time to fully embrace what they both needed. It was time to completely welcome back his Dom persona. He took a moment to let the feeling of dominance and power slide over him, like a favorite T-shirt that still fit just right.

"Never fear, my dear. Before the night is over, we will have put the whole ugly event behind us and you'll be forgiven. When we go home tomorrow, it'll be with a fresh start. We'll still have a lot of talking to do and we'll do that every night before bedtime. If I've learned nothing else, I've learned one of the most important parts of a D/s relationship is to communicate our own feelings openly. We need to understand each other's limits, our turn-ons and turn-offs. I'll tell you one thing right now though, and I pray to God you agree to this or we're going to have some serious problems."

"Anything, Markus. I'll do anything."

"Damn it, Brianna. You haven't been listening at all, have you? I don't want you to just agree with my ideas—*my* limits. I need to know what *you* want, what you *need*. If you aren't going be honest with me, then we'll find ourselves right back here again a few years from now. Do you hear me?" He realized too late he'd risen his voice.

The look of adoration shining in his wife's eyes as she smiled shyly back at him made his heart skip a beat. "You're right, Markus."

"If I'm right, why do you have that look on your face?"

Brianna broke into a huge grin. "Because you just totally sounded like a Dom and well, it made me all gooey inside."

His laugh filled the room. "Gooey, you say. Well, we have a few things to take care of before I can inspect your gooey spots." He hugged her close as she threw her arms around his neck, snuggling in to start kissing behind his ear before sucking on his earlobe. She knew how much that drove him crazy and it took all his willpower to separate them again. He loved how his sexy wife was breathing heavy, her desire for him shining clearly from her chocolate-brown eyes.

"Now, as I was saying. There's one thing we need to talk about first and foremost. I hope to hell you aren't looking for me to be your Dom 24/7, Brianna. As much as I am going to love being your Dom in our bedroom and under some other circumstances, I actually love sharing my life with you as my partner. I relish our long conversations about nothing and everything. I love that you share your opinions with me and tell me when you think

I'm being an ass. I don't ever want to dominate you to a point where you feel like you have to change who you are, because I *love* who you are. Do you hear me?"

Brianna threw her arms around him again, but this time she was talking against his neck while kissing him. "Oh Markus, that's the most wonderful, romantic thing you've ever said to me. That's exactly what I want, too, honey. I adore our life together. I don't want everything to change either. I just ... well ... in the bedroom, and when I'm naughty... I need..." Her words trailed off as she was once again unable to verbalize what she needed.

"It's okay, sweetheart. I may have been a little slow on the uptake, but now that you have my attention, I'm going to guide you. We'll figure out together what it is that you want—what you need."

The feel of her in his arms had stirred his cock to full attention and he was so tempted to roll her over and bury himself inside her again, but he knew that wasn't what either of them required most right now. He'd spent hours that afternoon, after Lukus had left, reading the domestic discipline websites Brianna had bookmarked as favorites. He knew his wife wanted him to lead her, to protect and discipline her when she deserved it. And without a doubt, he knew what he had to do before anything else. He peeled Brianna loose from his neck so he could look into her eyes.

He felt tangible relief seeing her passion for him shining.

I pray to God I'm reading her right and when I'm done, I'll see that same love shining back at me.

"Not yet, Bri. I feel it, too, but if you remember, I told you by the end of tonight, all will be forgiven, and we'll be able to have a fresh start. There's only one way to do that, sweetheart. I know you've been here at the club being punished for the last twenty-four hours by Lukus, and that I participated tonight, but if we're gonna put your infidelity behind us, then I need to punish you myself for putting our marriage in danger. I have to punish you for lying to me and, most importantly, for putting your own life in danger. You're the most important thing to me and you need to learn that I won't put up with you taking risks with your life."

The look in his wife's eyes was priceless. He wasn't sure how she pulled it off, but she had a strange mix of fear, excitement, and pride. He couldn't help but notice her breath was becoming labored as he watched her preparing mentally for what was to come. He half expected her to try to talk her way out of more punishment, so he was blown away when she quietly whispered, "Yes, Sir. Whatever you think is best, Sir."

Her submissive answer almost unmanned him. "Oh fuck, that's amazing hearing you say that, Brianna."

His long pushed-down dominance reared up as

he weaved both of his hands through her thick, messed, brunette hair and roughly yanked her to him to capture her lips in a powerful kiss. He felt his resolve slipping as her tongue invaded his mouth to tangle with his own and allowed them a few glorious minutes of making out like teenagers, before pulling away with a groan. Bri kept her eyes closed as she tried to catch her breath. It was hard for him to guess if she was more affected by the kiss or the impending punishment.

"Open your eyes, Brianna."

When she finally complied, he recognized it was the punishment weighing on her.

"Tonight, is going to be a more intimate punishment. You're going to be naked, over my lap and I'm going to spank you until I'm sure you've learned your lesson. I'm warning you now, this isn't going to be pleasant for you. I saw with my own eyes tonight how pain can affect you, and I can't wait to explore your limits with you, sweetheart. I can't wait to bring you so many amazing orgasms, but those won't be tonight. I know Lukus has already taught you that when you are being punished, you're not to come. It's supposed to hurt so you learn your lesson. If you come before I finish disciplining you, I'll have to start all over again. Do you understand me?"

Her lower lip trembled as she answered him quietly. "Yes, Sir. Can I ask a question before we start?"

"Of course, baby."

"Do I get a safeword for punishments?"

"That's a good question. You will, without a doubt, have a safeword for when we're playing. During a true punishment, I prefer to use the red-yellow system. If you need me to take a short break, you just need to say *yellow* and I'll let you catch your breath before we continue. If there is truly something wrong that you need me to stop then you can use *red*. But I warn you, if you use *red* just because you don't like the punishment, you're gonna be in bigger trouble with me. Do you understand?"

"Yes." He could hear the anticipation tinged with resignation in her voice.

"Time to lie over my lap now, sweetheart. For punishments, I'll always want you with your head on my left so I can use my stronger right hand to spank you."

As his beautiful wife situated herself over his lap, Markus was filled with a forgotten cocktail of feelings. He felt surges of both dominance and dread at the thought of having to discipline his wife. It was both better—and worse—preparing to punish Brianna than Georgie; Georgie was submissive in every way that she had almost never earned a real punishment. For that reason, almost all of their sessions had felt more like staged scenes, all part of the D/s game.

Tonight, seemed totally different. It was real.

Intimate. He couldn't deny that the Dom in him couldn't wait to feel his sexy wife wiggling across his lap, grinding into his cock as she learned her lesson. The powerful feelings coursing through him were intoxicating as he took a few minutes before starting to simply massage his wife's lower back, ass, and thighs, admiring the evidence of her previous punishments still visible across her bottom.

Overshadowing his sense of dominance was his feeling of responsibility to her—to protect, cherish, and guide her when she went off course, to punish her when she needed to learn an important lesson. The fact that she trusted him enough to play this important role in her life humbled him and he was surprised to find himself dreading having to actually hurt her. He'd always hated to hear Bri cry for any reason, and he knew he was going to have to harden his heart tonight against her impending tears.

This is what she craves, and you know it, Lambert. Hell, it's what you both need, so don't be such a pussy.

The first spank to her right butt cheek made Brianna flinch, and even though it wasn't necessarily that hard, she gasped. Plunging in, Markus delivered a quick dozen swats spread evenly across his wife's already pink ass. He was proud of her for not trying to squirm out of position or cover her bottom.

"Good girl, staying still. I forgot to tell you to

reach your hands out above your head on the bed. I don't want you to bring them back to your ass. I don't want to accidentally hurt your hand. Do you understand?"

She replied quietly. "Yes, Markus."

Giving her ass a sound spank, Markus reminded her. "During a punishment you will call me, 'Sir.'"

"Yes, Sir. I'm sorry, Sir."

Markus resumed a steady rhythm of hard, open-handed spanks as he lectured his wife to make sure she was learning her lesson. "Good girl. Now, Brianna, tell me again why you're being punished tonight."

"Because I cheated on you with Jake and put our marriage in danger."

He delivered several harder spanks to her ass, causing her to flinch and wiggle in his lap. "Yes. That's pretty serious, isn't it?"

"Yes, Sir. I'm so very sorry, Sir."

"I know you are. Why else are you being punished?"

"Because I lied to you."

As the loud, steady whacking sound of hard spanks filled the room, her wiggling became worse, but so far she'd been able to keep her hands above her as he'd told her to.

"That's right. I won't tolerate lies, Brianna. You'll be severely punished each and every time I find out you lied to me. Is that understood?"

"Oh, God! Yes, Sir. I understand."

Markus heard the quaver in her voice and could detect she might start to cry. He hated that he could feel his cock beginning to throb as it was trapped beneath her wiggling tummy. It felt so wrong that he was getting turned on by her vulnerability, at least up until he heard the telltale moan that escaped his lovely wife after a particularly fast volley of spanks to her sensitive sit-spot.

"Brianna Nicole Lambert, you had best not be getting close to coming, do you hear me?"

"Oh please, Markus. I've dreamed of you spanking me like this for so long now that I'm so turned on. Please, can't I come?"

He couldn't help but chuckle. "Oh, I think I'm in big trouble here. I can see I'm gonna have to come up with some other creative ways to punish you that you don't like. Either that or you're going to start being naughty just so you can get a sound, hard spanking on this beautiful bottom of yours. You will not come. Not yet. We aren't even close to done yet."

Her frustrated groan made him smile. He spent the next few minutes alternating between fast volleys of hard swats spread all over her beautiful ass and stopping to massage her lower back, giving her short breaks to collect herself. Like Lukus, he was a firm believer there should be no rubbing away the pain of a true punishment, so when she finally tried to reach back to rub her burning ass during one of the breaks, he quickly snatched her hand away and delivered a fast dozen swats to her most sensitive spot where her ass met her thighs.

"You will not rub during a punishment," he said sternly. "I know Lukus has already warned you about that. I suggest you remember from now on."

Her reply was breathy. "But, Sir. It hurts so bad."

"I know it does, baby. Are you learning your lesson?"

"Oh yes, Sir. I really am."

"That's good. We have just one more lesson to learn tonight and then your punishment will be over and we can put all of this behind us forever."

Markus gently lifted his wife off his lap so he could lean over and dig into the nightstand drawer. He knew Lukus always kept an assortment of toys, lubes, and punishment devices stored close to the bed for just such occasions. He was very happy to find one of his favorite punishment implements on top in the drawer.

Brianna's eyes widened when she saw the heavy wooden hairbrush her husband pulled out of the drawer. It was larger than a normal hairbrush and he could see she understood it was made for one purpose—to teach wayward submissives and wives to behave. Markus had to harden his heart against the tears falling freely down her cheeks. He reached out to hold her hand, intimately entwining his fingers with hers.

"I'm going to spank you with the hairbrush now, Brianna, to teach you the most important lesson. Without a doubt, the biggest mistake you made was putting your life in danger by going anywhere with that asshole. He's proven he enjoys hurting you. As angry as I am that you cheated on me, it's the fact you were stupid enough to risk your life that scares me the most. I know it's harsh, sweetheart, but I need to know you'll never do such a dangerous thing ever again."

"I promise, Markus. I really have already learned that lesson. I know it was totally stupid and reckless and I'm so very sorry."

Markus brought her hand up to his lips and spent a few seconds kissing her palm. He could see in her eyes that she was hoping he was going to relent and stop the punishment that he knew he must continue. She was testing his resolve, but they were setting the groundwork for the future. She needed to know if they were going to live a D/s lifestyle, that there were consequences for her actions. He pulled her back over his lap.

"Time to get this over with so we can go back to making up. I want you to hold onto the edge of the bed and not let go, sweetheart. I know it's going to be hard for you not to try to interfere once I get started."

Markus heard a forlorn moan escape from his

wife as she reached forward, stretching out to grasp the edge of the bed. He could see her holding it tightly, bracing herself. She was already breathing heavily, and he hadn't even started yet.

The sound of the wooden hairbrush connecting with Brianna's ass surprised them both. Markus knew right away he needed to be careful not to overdo it because it was heavy. He didn't want to leave bruises. By the third swat, Brianna was already crying out loud.

"Oh please, Sir! It's too much! It hurts so bad! Please stop!"

Markus had a lump in his throat as he continued to pelt his wife's ass, knowing they both needed this to be a memorable punishment so they could truly put this whole damn nightmare behind them. With each swat, her crying grew stronger until she was sobbing. He pushed through his reticence, listening carefully for a safeword and relieved when he heard none.

He'd never been a big fan of counting swats, so he had no idea exactly how many he'd delivered with the unyielding brush; he figured it was at least several dozen. He'd tuned into the sounds his wife was making as she struggled to maintain her position, recognizing he was nearing the end of the punishment when he heard her crying out her repentance.

"I am so sorry, so very sorry, Sir. I promise... I really promise..." Her voice trailed off as the next fast volley of swats connected hard with her sit spot, spreading a memorable line of fire across her punished ass. This time her plea came out in an almost scream.

"I swear to you Markus. I promise!"

All resistance to her punishment left with that scream. Brianna's body went limp in total submission as he delivered the final dozen swats to her roasted butt with a heavy thud. Markus stopped, putting the hairbrush down on the bed where she could see it. He reached out to stroke her back to comfort her before wiping away some of her tears.

"Tell me, Brianna. What do you promise?"

Through her continued crying she told him. "I promise I will never... *ever*... go anywhere with Jake again."

"What are you gonna do if he ever makes contact with you again?"

"I'm going to tell you right away and then," she had to pause to gasp through a sob before finishing, "I'm going to call the police," she wailed.

"Good girl. And why was your punishment so much worse for this than actually cheating on me?"

Her cathartic crying had slowed, and she answered through whimpers and hiccups. "Because I put myself in danger."

"Very good. You're the most important thing in my life, Brianna. If anything ever happens to you, I'll never forgive myself. That means you need to be careful to never knowingly put yourself in danger."

Markus helped Brianna back into his lap. He heard her sharp intake of breath when her punished ass hit his bare legs. Heat radiated from her bottom as he hugged her close. She put her head on his shoulder, nestling into the crook of his neck as she recovered. A wave of sheer bliss washed over him as he realized just how lucky he was. As shitty as this whole situation had been, he knew things could have turned out so much worse.

When he pulled back so he could wipe away her tears, he saw the all-consuming passion in her eyes. No matter how much the spanking had hurt, without a doubt the submissive part of his wife had loved every single minute of her intimate time over his lap.

God damn I'm gonna have fun training her. I have to be the luckiest damn man on the planet.

"Now, Mrs. Lambert. I seem to remember talk of some gooey spots that might need some attention from your husband."

Brianna's eyes grew dark with a sexual hunger as Markus snaked his right hand between her legs, pushing slowly upward. When he reached his intended target, he couldn't help but chuckle.

"Wow, Mrs. Lambert. I do believe you have a small problem here. You seem to have sprung a leak because you're absolutely soaking wet. If I didn't know any better, I would say you were in need of some attention from your husband, but I don't know how that could be possible considering I've serviced you twice in just the last few hours. Tell me, what exactly is it you need?"

Markus wished he had a camera so he could capture the expression on Brianna's face as she formulated her response. He'd truly never seen her look more stunning than she did that very minute. She was a hot mess, with her dark hair tousled, her lips swollen from kisses and tear tracks still visible down her cheeks. He paused, committing the image to memory although he was sure he'd see her like this again.

"Oh Markus, please honey, I need you inside me." She was pleading urgently now. "I need you to fuck me, right now. Take me hard and fast like you did on the stage. It felt so good and it made me know without a doubt that I belong to you. That's what I want more than anything else. Fuck me like you own me."

Markus's erection was already uncomfortably rigid, and her wanton behavior was threatening to undo him. With what little shred of control he had left, he managed to lift Bri off his lap. Moving up to his knees, he maneuvered her onto her hands and knees facing the headboard.

"Reach out and hold onto the headboard rails, sweetheart. That's it. Head down so you're sticking that exquisite ass out for me. I'm gonna take you long and hard from behind and as I do, you're going to feel my body slamming against your blistered butt with every thrust, reminding you that you're mine. Mine alone to love, to fuck, discipline, protect, cherish."

"I love you so much, Markus." He heard her whispered reply and his own heart did a very un-Dom-like flip-flop.

Markus quickly got her positioned the way he wanted before he lined up his hard tool and shoved balls-deep into his wife's hot, wet cunt in one powerful thrust. They both cried out at the suddenness of their coupling. Markus set a fast, hard pace while he grabbed Brianna's hips so he could pull her back to meet his thrusts, driving as deep into her as he possibly could. In his possessiveness, he wanted to touch places inside her he'd never touched before. He was determined to reclaim her in every way.

He could hear her as she let loose a lusty ramble. "Oh fuck, yeah. This is exactly what I needed, honey. Take me hard. I'm yours. You own me."

Markus could feel the walls of her pussy clenching his cock tightly as her first fiery orgasm rolled through. Because he'd come twice in the last few hours, he was gratefully able to hold his own release off for several long, intense minutes. He leaned over Bri's back and alternated tweaking her clit and nipples, bringing her to two more powerful orgasms that finally pushed her to scream out to her husband.

"Please Markus, you need to come inside me now. I don't know how much more I can take before I pass out. You feel so fucking good pounding me like this, but I need you to come. Please, shoot your cum inside me, honey."

He didn't need any more encouragement. His wife's naughty rant had him shooting ropes of cum inside her. A long manly grunt escaped as he remained buried, waiting to deposit every last drop as deep as possible so she could feel his cum dripping out of her while they slept snuggled up for the rest of the night.

As soon as he could think clearly again, he maneuvered them both until they were lying down as he spooned her from behind, his cock still deep in her pussy. He knew it was just a matter of time before his dick would be soft enough to slip out of her slick folds, but he was determined to enjoy every minute until then nestled inside of his wife. They spent a few minutes in quiet reflection as the final candle flickered out, casting them into darkness. It was almost as if it knew its job was now done.

Just before he drifted off into a deep sleep, Markus heard his wife whisper. "I love you, Markus."

"Not even close to as much as I love you, Brianna. Get some sleep now, sweetheart." His sentence wasn't even finished when he heard the slow, steady breathing of his already sleeping wife.

Yep. I'm the luckiest bastard on the face of the Earth. I didn't even know I was missing anything, but now I know for a fact that I'm one of the lucky few who get to have it all in life.

CHAPTER TWO

LUKUS

"Jesus Christ, woman! You're killing me here. Have you no shame whatsoever? Are you trying to humiliate me completely?"

Lukus was having trouble catching his breath from the workout Tiffany had just put him through for the last thirty minutes. Even though he worked out hard a couple times a week, now he found himself bent from the stitch in his ribs.

The sound of Tiffany's victorious laughter should've pissed him off, but he was too fucking impressed to be mad. He finally managed to catch his breath as he stood upright to take in the sight of her a few feet away, the most beautiful smile on her sweat-covered face. Despite being too large for her, the t-shirt he loaned her was clinging to her damp curves in all the right places.

"The worst part is that you managed that without any shoes on. Barefoot. You just beat me *barefoot.* If the security crew finds out about this, I'll never hear the end of it. I'm not sure what it's gonna take, but I'll pay any price for your silence. This has to stay our little secret or I'll never live it down."

Her intoxicating laughter was so feminine, reminding him she was still the same woman he'd met twelve hours before.

"I think you're being a bit melodramatic, Lukus. Don't you? Maybe instead of paying me off, you should let me at them, too. That should shut 'em up."

"Oh, hell no. No one's going to play with you except me, you got that? I let you loose on those guys and they'll try to move in and steal you away from me. Nope. We're just gonna keep you my secret weapon for now. I'll figure out exactly when the right time is to unleash you on them."

Tiffany braved moving closer, reaching out with her index finger to touch a droplet of sweat on Lukus's neck and then gently traced it with her finger as it rolled down his bare, muscular chest. She took a few minutes to admire his pecs and impressive six-pack.

Lukus watched her carefully as she admired his well-toned body. She must've realized she had zoned out in her adoration because she quickly glanced up to see if he was watching her. As their eyes met, he could see the fire burning in her gaze.

He was glad their little unplanned detour hadn't put out their flame.

The smile on her face had changed from playful to predatory. "Maybe you shouldn't have given me the full tour after all, Lukus."

"I deserved this. I thought you'd be impressed that my place was big enough to have a basketball court. How the hell could I possibly know you were Michael Fucking Jordan in a dress? Where the hell did you learn to play like that?"

Her light-hearted laughter was back. "You know, for a security guru who has a whole stable of private investigators, you really did a terrible job of digging into my history. I'm very disappointed in you, Lukus." Her mischievous taunt had exactly the effect on Lukus he suspected she'd intended.

"Well, I'm sorry I disappointed you, but considering I only met you less than twelve hours ago, I'd hope you'd cut me a bit of slack. I'm sure I can have a detailed dossier prepared on you by morning. But then again..."

He took great joy in watching her reaction as he inched closer until he finally reached out, grabbing her hips and pulling her tight against his overheated body. He couldn't give a shit they were both in need of a hot shower. He wanted her to feel his quickly growing erection straining for escape from his gym shorts.

"Maybe I should go old school. Who needs computers and the Internet for investigative work?

I could just take you to my room and start with a nice, thorough strip search."

Lukus stopped long enough to lean in and seductively kiss her behind her ear. He felt a tremor race through her as his lips touched her skin. He kept kissing down her neck as he continued with his teasing threats. "I could tie you down, torture you for hours until you finally couldn't resist me anymore. I am a professional, after all. I'm sure I can make you spill all your secrets."

Lukus loved the long, drawn-out groan he was able to drag out of his beautiful captive. He felt her leaning on him heavily, as if her legs were going weak beneath her, just as she threw her arms around his neck for support.

Lukus fought the urge to throw her down to the hardwood and take her right there on the free-throw line. "As much as I'd like to see where this is headed, I think we're both due a long, hot shower. I'm afraid I need a few minutes alone to lick my wounds from being soundly whipped at basketball —and by a barefoot girl no less."

Tiffany pulled back so she could look up into his smoldering eyes. "I resent that. In case you haven't noticed, I'm a woman."

Lukus couldn't help but burst out laughing. He took great joy in bending to lift her over his shoulder in a fireman's hold, much like he had done out in the alley earlier. "Oh, baby, there's no chance in hell I missed that you're all woman. But just to be sure, I'd better do some pretty thorough investigating after our shower—you know—just to make sure." Lukus couldn't resist slapping her elevated ass, drawing a wonderful squeal from Tiff that shot straight to his hard cock.

Just hang on a bit longer there, sport. I have a feeling we're finally going to get lucky here pretty soon.

Lukus walked them through the loft, which was dim except for a few low lights and the glow of the Chicago skyline sifting in through the floor-to-ceiling wall of windows in the great room. In the master suite, he deposited Tiffany in his bathroom. He briefly contemplated ripping off the damn T-shirt and carrying her into the oversized shower to ravish her under the showerheads. He suspected she'd be more than willing, but something told him not to rush it, not with this one.

"So, you take this bathroom, Tiff. You can have a nice soak in the tub, although the shower is really awesome, if I do say so myself. I'm going to go clean up in the guest bathroom. I'll lay out a fresh T-shirt for you on the bed. I'll meet you in the theater with some snacks and drinks. Anything special you want?"

The surprise on Tiffany's face told him she'd been expecting him to stay and shower with her. She recovered. "Whatever you have is great, although it looks like you could use a Gatorade."

She smiled mischievously before continuing. "Honestly, I wouldn't mind a glass of wine if you have anything good."

"Damn. I forgot to show you the wine closet in the pantry on the tour. I knew I was forgetting something."

"Show-off."

"Damn straight. I spent a small fortune on all this stuff. I knew it would come in handy one day when I was finally ready to impress a girl."

"Woman. Impress a woman."

"We'll see. I'll reserve judgment until my full-body inspection is complete." He flashed her his most devilish smile.

"Smart-ass."

"Sass. You're just full of sass, aren't you, Miss O'Sullivan?"

Her eyes sparkled as she displayed her flirtatious smile. "Well, when you swim with the sharks, you need to stay on your toes. I'd hate to get bitten."

"Never fear, baby. I hadn't planned on biting. Nibbling, yes. Biting, no. We're not quite ready for that anyway, unless of course you're into that sort of thing. Now, I can't promise other slightly painful things won't happen to this fabulous body of yours, but I do promise this—you're gonna love them all."

Her only answer to his naughty promise was a quietly whispered, "Oh, my freaking God."

Lukus couldn't resist leaning in and planting a

tender kiss on her surprised lips before pulling back and heading to leave. Just as he was ready to close the door behind him, he got the last word in. "Don't take too long now, Tiffany. We haven't discussed punishments for tardiness yet. I'll be not-so-patiently waiting in the theater."

Lukus

Lukus closed the door quietly behind him and leaned against it to take a deep breath.

I'm so in over my head here. She's fucking amazing, beautiful, intelligent, funny... Michael Fucking Jordan.

He finally pulled it together enough to grab them both a change of clothes before heading to the guest bathroom. He entered through the middle guest room, happy to see Derek and Rachel hadn't totally messed it up with their earlier *naptime*. As he opened the door to the bathroom, he was startled to see Markus standing naked with his back to him at the toilet, taking a whiz.

"I didn't expect to see you tonight. Especially, *all* of you."

Markus flinched at the sound of his best friend's voice before chuckling. "Can't a guy take a piss without getting interrupted around here?"

"I'm amazed you were able to pry yourself out

of your wife long enough to piss. I thought you'd be balls-deep all night."

Having finished, Markus turned around, a sly smile on his face. "Careful. I've decided to pace myself. My wife is more than satisfied. She's sleeping like a baby after getting her bedtime punishment spanking along with several make-up sessions. Thanks for leaving the hairbrush in the nightstand. By the way, tomorrow I need to pick your brain for some creative punishments she's actually not going to like."

Lukus chuckled. "You're really going to have your hands full, you lucky bastard."

Markus got serious as he answered his friend. "I know I am and honestly, I have a favor to ask you, Lukus. Let's face it. You were right earlier when you said I'd been a shitty Dom to Georgie. I've given it thought and... well... I love Bri so much and I owe it to her to make sure I get my shit together."

Lukus tried to lighten the mood. "Let's not get mushy, now."

"I'm serious. I know it's lame, but would you consider giving me some coaching? I mean, you know me better than anyone else other than Bri. And now that you know Bri, I suspect you have a handle on what direction I need to take her training. Think you could spend some time working up a plan with me?"

Lukus was shocked at the candid and heartfelt request from his best friend.

"Wow. Who are you, and what'd you do with Markus?"

"Fuck you."

"Seriously, Markus. I never thought you'd ask me for help. You've always preferred to be the *helper* rather than the *helpee*. At the risk of sounding like a pompous ass, I'm proud of you. I know we've spent a lot of time together over the last year because of the trial, but I don't think I'm telling you anything you don't already know. Things still haven't really felt the same as it was before, well, before that night. I really am sorry Bri cheated on you, but I can't tell you how much it means to me that you asked me for my help. It feels like the old days, and I like it."

"Yeah, me too," Markus replied. "I just wish I hadn't had to get hit over the head with a fucking sledgehammer to wake me up. But I guess I need to get back to my wife." Markus narrowed his eyes at his friend. "What the hell are you doing in this bathroom, anyway?"

"I just need a quick shower. Tiffany's using my bathroom."

"And you aren't in there with her? I saw the way you were looking at her tonight. You want to fuck her."

"Hey, watch it. I do want to fuck her, but..."

"But, what?" Markus's eyes lit up with mischief as he caught on. "But, she's knocking you on your ass, isn't she? I can see it in your eyes."

Lukus wanted so bad to deny it, but his best friend was exactly right.

"Fuck. Is this how you felt when you met Brianna? Let's face it. I've spent next to no time whatsoever with non-subs like Tiff. I've known for some time now I was getting bored with the subs that would come and go here at the club. It's almost like I've been waiting for something to change, but I had no fucking clue what it was. Now I meet a woman who's a one-eighty from any woman I've gone out with since my senior prom and she has me acting like that eighteen-year-old all over again because I'm so worried I'm gonna scare her away."

Markus chuckled. "Oh man, you do have it bad. I'd love to offer some advice that could make it easier, but you're talking to the guy who just forgave his wife for cheating on him with her psychotic ex-boyfriend because he can't live without her."

The men lapsed into silence for a moment before Lukus quietly asked his next question. "Was it worth it? Turning in your Dom card, I mean?"

"Hell, yes. I'd do it again in a heartbeat if that's what it took to make Bri happy. It wasn't so bad. Sure, I had to give up some things, but what I gained was so much better."

"And now you get the full package. Bri wants a Dom after all." Lukus hated that he could hear the tinge of bitterness in his own voice.

"And who says you can't have the same thing?"

"I don't know, Markus. Tiffany isn't Bri. She's a total newbie to the whole scene. I can tell it scares the shit out of her. Who am I kidding? *I* scare the shit out of her."

He stopped talking to stare at his friend. "What the hell are you smiling at?"

"You. Lukus Mitchell—the Master's Master— needs help navigating the tricky waters with a new sub."

"Very funny. Haven't you been listening? Tiffany isn't a submissive."

"No, Lukus. Haven't *you* been listening? You already have your answer. You're just too close to see it. Don't make the same fucking mistake I made. Tiffany wants to explore her submissive feelings just like Brianna does. They loan each other their iPads loaded up with BDSM love stories. They love the same bookmarked websites and blogs on domestic discipline and the whole D/s lifestyle. They both went to the BDSM clubs together years ago.

"The only difference between the two of them is that Brianna actually met someone in the lifestyle—or someone she thought was in the lifestyle. Unfortunately, Tiffany ended up with a front row seat to Brianna's abuse and they both ended up scarred in the process.

"I've known Tiff as long as I've known Bri. She was there the night I met Brianna at the benefit dinner and I'm telling you—you'll need to go slow with her and give her time to learn that what she saw between Jake and Brianna wasn't what BDSM is all about. She's a lot like Brianna—she's confused by her submissive feelings but doesn't know how to talk about it. You'll need to guide her with baby steps."

Lukus grew dark. "I could fucking kill that bastard, Jake. It was bad enough when I knew what he did to Bri, but seeing how it's affected Tiff, too? Let's just say it's a good thing you're on retainer, buddy, because if I manage to bump into him, I'm gonna beat the shit out of him."

"Funny you should mention it. I was gonna let the dust settle for a few days and then come hire you to dig up everything you can on the fucker. I'm going after the little prick, Lukus. I should have done it years ago, but Bri talked me out of it. He's a menace and someone needs to put him down. I'm not talking contract killer shit here. I just need information I can use to destroy him and put him behind bars. You know damn well he's hurting other women, too."

"Fuck yeah," Lukus said. "But you don't need to hire me. I'll do it for free."

"If things work out with Tiff, you'll have as much at stake as I do." Markus started to head back towards his bedroom. "Take your shower. We'll talk tomorrow. I need to get back to my wife."

"Don't you mean your submissive?"

Markus turned back to face his best friend.

"No. Bri is my wife first and foremost. Since it seems you might be on the verge of following my footsteps into domestic bliss, I should warn you Lukus. Neither Bri nor Tiff will ever be full-timers and honestly, I wouldn't have it any other way. I love how strong Brianna is. I already told her tonight that while she may be my sub in the bedroom and I may be the head of our household, I refuse to dominate her to the point that she changes who she is. And you'll need to be careful, too. If you're looking to turn Tiff into a 24/7 sub, do us all a favor and walk away now. As mad as I was at her yesterday, I love Tiffany. She's pretty special just the way she is." He paused to study his friend. "Are you going to be happy with an equal partner outside of the bedroom?"

"If you'd asked me that question a week ago, I'm not sure what my answer would've been. But tonight, I came to the same conclusion." He couldn't stop himself from breaking into a shit-eating grin. "She has this sass about her—a fire I find myself attracted to."

"Holy shit. I'm totally blown away. You aren't even trying to deny it."

"What's the point? We had an argument over a fucking brownie this afternoon and the most surprising part was that I loved every minute of it. What the hell is *that* all about? I should probably be freaking out over how quickly she's gotten under my skin, but if I'm halfway honest with myself, I haven't had this much fun around a woman in a long time."

Markus was laughing again. "This is gonna be entertaining. I'm not exactly sure who's going to be training whom."

"Very funny. Hey, before you leave, I have one more question. Where the hell did she learn to play basketball like Michael Fucking Jordan?"

"Oh, Jesus. Don't tell me that's why you need a shower? Don't ever play against her. You'll lose every damn time. Believe me. I learned the hard way."

"Too late. She already whipped my ass. So, how did she get so good?"

"You didn't ask her?"

Lukus smiled a sly smile. "We were a little busy."

"Right. Well I'll let her give you all the details, but she had a full ride scholarship to play women's basketball at the University of Michigan. It's where she and Bri met and were roommates for four years. She got good because she comes from a large Irish-Italian Catholic family. She has a boatload of athletic brothers, almost all of them cops if I remember correctly." Markus started to chuckle. "Now that I think of it, I'd be careful if I were you. They've always been pretty protective of her."

Lukus let out a full groan. "Fucking great. That's just what I need. A boatload of protective cops breathing down my neck."

"Hey, it could be worse. They could all be lawyers like me."

"Well, that's the truth."

Markus headed towards the door then turned to look back at his friend. "Hey. I just want to say thanks again for all that you did for Bri and me the last few days. I know I've been a complete and utter ass to you where she was concerned and well... I just want you to know I'm sorry and I truly do hope you can give me a chance to make it up to you."

"It's okay, Markus. I didn't understand until I met Brianna, but it makes sense now. Just don't ever try to pull some shit like that on me again."

"Deal. Night and good luck with Tiff. I think you're gonna need it."

Yeah, I think I'm gonna need it too.

Tiffany

Tiffany knew she'd been stalling long enough. If she didn't get going soon, Lukus was going to come looking for her and when he did, it would only take him two seconds flat to realize he'd made a mistake leaving her alone in his room.

What the hell am I doing? I'm going to get my heart broken for sure. There's no way in hell someone like Lukus is going to be happy with someone like me.

Tiff had been so excited to go join Lukus in the theater that she had sped through her shower, barely taking time to wash her long, blonde hair. And even though he'd left her a new toothbrush, she'd used his instead. She knew it was childish to want to share his toothbrush, but something about it seemed so intimate.

Curious and wanting a bit of fun, she'd even spent a few moments rifling through his bathroom cabinets, subconsciously looking for clues into the mystery of Master Lukus Mitchell. And it *had* been fun, right up until she opened the cabinet holding all of the tools of his Dom trade.

I should have listened to my mother. She's always told me curiosity killed the cat.

As hard as she'd tried, Tiffany hadn't been able to slow her heart rate since spending several long minutes inspecting each and every item in that cabinet. She'd taken the time to evaluate how each implement made her feel and finally came to the conclusion that while a few toys—like the paddles and the fleece-lined wrist and ankle cuffs—had turned her on, most of the items just plain scared the shit out of her.

Sure, she'd always enjoyed racy romance novels that included scenes featuring anal plugs, fierce nipple clamps, and other bondage devices. But in reality, the closest she'd ever gotten to them was as a spectator in the BDSM clubs years ago with Brianna. Even then, the club scene had always had an air of theater. She'd very much enjoyed being a witness to naughty subs being punished and played with in all sorts of creative or even artistic, ways. The visions stuck with her and even years later, she could still conjure those memories as if they had happened yesterday.

But here in Lukus's private space, the sex toys were real. She'd touched them and she had no choice but to confront how she really felt about the possibility of his using them on her. For that matter —and she hated to admit it—she was going to have to confront how she really felt about his having used them on others before her. She suspected it was many others and that caused her a moment of near panic.

How is he ever going to be happy with me when he can have so many other women who aren't afraid to let him do whatever he wants with them. If he thinks he's ever going to give me a damn punishment enema, he has another think coming.

Tiff finally forced herself to leave the bathroom and finish dressing. Sitting on his bed, she tried to calm herself. She wasn't sure if it was helping or hurting, but she hugged Lukus's pillow to her face, enjoying his masculine scent that lingered there. She forced herself to remember Brianna's words earlier in the day—how in spite of all of the punishments Lukus had layered on her, Brianna's trust for him had grown. Tiff recalled the unwavering trust Brianna placed in Lukus, even forgiving him tonight after he and Markus had tested her resolve to be faithful to her husband.

Why can't I trust him, too? He hasn't done anything that's hurt me.

That was when it hit her. It was as if Brianna was right in the room, admonishing Tiff for always trying to make things harder than they needed to be.

Tiff and Bri had always been good chess players. While thinking strategically may have been key to the game of chess, Brianna was the one who finally recognized that Tiff had the nasty habit of trying to think so far ahead in her relationships that she would often torpedo men without even giving them a fair chance, simply because she suspected the *game* wouldn't turn out as she'd planned. It was as if she wanted to strategically plan out her next three moves on the board at the beginning of a new relationship to make sure the moves she was making were the right ones.

Brianna had told her over and over that being in a relationship wasn't like chess—a game they both loved—and Tiffany knew her friend was right when she told her she couldn't plan all the moves in life ahead of time. People weren't pieces on a board, and where the rules of chess were rigid, the rules of the relationship game were not fixed. They changed. Tiff's tendency to keep one step ahead was not only a waste of time, but could be destructive.

Hell, Lukus himself said it tonight when he asked me, "Please, can't you at least give us half a chance before you throw it away?"

Tiff recalled what she felt earlier as—bound and helpless—she was made to watch Brianna's punishment. In her mind's eye, she could still see the men working together on stage to bring Brianna such pain, but also such pleasure. She recalled the sound of the riding crop as it whizzed through the air before snapping against Bri's already tender skin, the sight of Markus fucking Brianna so punishingly hard and fast on the stage floor, the sound of their cries betraying just how much they loved each other.

She realized what she was feeling now at these memories was not fear, but excitement. And that excitement grew as she remembered the feel of Lukus's erection pressed against her as they shared their first kiss—a kiss that had somehow felt different than any other before. Afterwards he'd made a startling confession, that he was as off-balance as she was about whatever was happening between them.

As she took another long drag of his scent from the pillow, she knew it really came down to only two choices. She could either sneak out now and leave with her heart safely intact and go back to being a voyeur into this lifestyle, or she could jump into the deep end of the pool and trust that Lukus would be there to catch her so that the two of them could navigate these new depths together.

It's just one night. If ever I've wanted to explore, surely tonight is my chance. If he pushes me to try something I don't want, I'll just say no. Hopefully he'll listen. Wait. No. I know he'll listen. I saw it with my own eyes. He's careful. He's not Jake. He won't let anything hurt me. And anyway, Bri and Markus are right next door if I need help.

Now that she'd thought things through, she couldn't help but smile with relief.

Well, that was easy. There's no way I'm prepared to get in my car and drive away from him, not tonight. Not after what he said to me down on the stage. It looks like I'm going swimming.

Energized, Tiff jumped up, ready to head out to the theater. Then she caught a vision of herself standing there in the oversized Harley-Davidson T-shirt Lukus had laid out for her along with a pair of his boxer briefs.

Oh, hell no.

She returned to the bathroom for more primping, coaxing her semi-dry hair into a casual, sexy style. Then she headed to Lukus's closet. It only took her a minute to find what she was looking for. Slipping the Harley T-shirt off, Tiff reached out to pull one of Lukus's button-down dress shirts from its hanger. She was pleased that it hung low enough to cover her ass and just a few inches of her toned legs. She buttoned just a few strategic buttons in the middle, careful to leave enough undone to give Lukus peeks of what she was hiding underneath. She loosely rolled up the sleeves, luxuriating in how the soft linen felt against her body.

After admiring her look in the nearby floor-length mirror, Tiff made one final wardrobe change. Feeling a surge of naughty empowerment, she slid off the boxers, leaving them along with the t-shirt on the floor for Lukus to find later.

Okay, Lukus. Ready or not, here I come. Please, be gentle with me.

CHAPTER THREE

LUKUS

Lukus was just about to crawl out of his skin after waiting for what seemed like an eternity for Tiffany to join him in the theater. He'd distracted himself by making popcorn and going through his movie collection to find the films he and Tiffany talked about earlier. He figured he'd let her choose her favorite, since he planned on spending the whole night watching her instead of the movie anyway. He'd already dimmed the lights for a romantic setting.

He was behind the bar mixing a Jack and Coke when he caught movement out of the corner of his eye. He glanced up as he poured the Coke to welcome Tiff to the theater and froze.

"Fuck me." A low growl accompanied his expletive. He stood frozen in place as he caught his first glimpse of Tiffany just inside the door to the room. She was definitely *not* in the Harley T-shirt he'd left out on the bed. In fact, courtesy of the side lamp she was standing directly in front of, he could see she was definitely *not* wearing his boxer shorts either. The back lighting was perfectly outlining her very curvy, very naked, body through his now favorite dress shirt.

She's so fucking hot. I'm gonna remember this moment every time I wear that shirt.

"Ah, damn it." Lukus had no choice but to tear his attention away from Tiff as the Coke he was pouring overflowed the glass, making a mess on the bar. He could hear Tiffany giggling as he reached to grab a bar towel to try to sop up the drink before it dripped onto the carpet. Only when he had the spill contained did he glance back up to see Tiffany walking slowly towards him, a totally naughty smile on her face. She took a seat on the high barstool across from him.

"What's the problem, Lukus? Looks like you're making a mess back there. Are you sure you know what you're doing?" Her voice was soft and playful.

"I'm not sure about me, but I can see by that twinkle in your eye, young lady, that you *absolutely* know what you're doing, you little minx."

Suddenly looking nervous, Tiffany quietly answered, "Don't be so sure. Looks can be deceiving. Truthfully, I feel so nervous that I've nearly forgotten why I'm still here."

Her vulnerability cut through his chest like a knife. Leaning forward to place his forearms on the bar, Lukus moved in closer to stare into her ocean-blue eyes before answering her in a voice that left no room for doubt. "Well then. Let me remind you. You're here because this is exactly where you belong tonight. I know it. You know it. I just wish you'd stop fighting it, baby."

"Easy for you to say. This is your house. This is just another day for you." She took a short break. He could see she was debating if she really wanted to continue on with her thought. He patiently waited her out until she finally continued. "I don't think you have a clue just how close I came to putting my dress back on and sneaking out to my car."

Even in the dim lighting, it was easy for Lukus to see her uncertainty was back. He stood and walked around the end of the bar until he was directly behind her barstool. Tiff made no attempt to turn herself around to face him, so Lukus took the opportunity to reach out and smooth down a few escaped wisps of her silky hair. He finally swiveled her barstool around so that she was facing him.

He leaned forward, placing his hands on either side of her on the backrest, effectively trapping her. Lukus leaned his body forward against her, happy when she subconsciously opened her legs to draw him in as he pressed close. When their faces were just a few inches apart, Tiffany quickly closed her eyes, apparently deciding his stare was too intense.

"Open your eyes, Tiffany." When she didn't comply, Lukus reached up to cup her cheek with his hand, stroking her gently with his thumb. When he detected her leaning slightly into his hand, seeking out his intimacy, he repeated his request. "Open your eyes, baby... please." His voice was soft, careful not to spook her.

When Tiffany finally opened her eyes, he could see the glossy sheen of her tears. He continued to speak gently. "First, thank you for being honest with me about wanting to leave. This will never work if you hide your feelings from me. Now, if you feel uncomfortable at my place, that's okay. I can fix that. I can take you home to your place or to a neutral downtown hotel with lots of wonderful amenities to spoil you. Just tell me where you'll feel comfortable and I'll make it happen. But walking away is not an option, Tiffany. I won't allow that to happen. I'm not letting you out of my sight until we can get a handle on whatever the hell it is that's happening between us."

When she remained silent, he continued. "And for the record, you couldn't be more wrong. The fact you think this is just a normal day for me just proves you don't know me as well as you seem to think you do. Maybe—just maybe—you should give me the benefit of the doubt until I prove I don't deserve it. You think you can do that?"

He could see the hope flicker in her eyes. He detected her slight nod as her only reply.

"So, where's all that sass now, Miss O'Sullivan?" he asked, grinning. "You've got me hooked on your beautiful, sassy mouth. Don't tell me you're all out of jibes for me."

He knew he'd succeeded at breaking through her defenses when Tiff's shy smile returned.

"Oh, don't worry. I'll never run out of sass. Maybe I'm just being careful to use it more wisely. After all, I'm not entirely sure I understand all the rules of the game we're playing."

Lukus was suddenly serious again. "Oh baby, that's your whole problem. This isn't a game, at least not for me. Nothing has felt this real to me in a very long time."

Tiff sucked in a sharp breath, surprised by his admission. "Why me, Lukus? Seriously..."

Lukus moved his fingers to her lips, effectively shushing her. "Stop. Enough analyzing. We have plenty of time for that later. Tonight, let it be enough to know it's because you look amazing in my favorite shirt."

Tiff's mischievous smile told him she was pleased. "This is really your favorite shirt?"

Lukus's smile turned predatory. "It is now," he said, and watched surprise flicker in her eyes. As their gaze remained locked, Lukus expertly sought out the few buttons holding his *favorite* shirt closed. He felt lower, unbuttoning each button slowly until none remained.

He loved watching the emotions parade

through her expressive eyes as he slowly opened the dress shirt wide, exposing her luscious body to him. Without breaking their passion-fueled visual connection, he moved his hands lower slowly, grasping her bare ass and not so gently pulled her body forward to the edge of the stool, bringing her now naked core hard against his straining erection, the fabric of his jeans the only thing separating them.

Tiff took a deep breath, her penetrating stare turned to liquid heat as he reached up to gently cup her heavy breasts in his two hands, flicking his thumbs lightly over each peak. A wave of power surged through Lukus as he witnessed the effect he was having on her—the feel of her nipples hardening at his touch, the rise and fall of her chest as her breath became labored with sexual excitement, the sweep of her tongue subconsciously wetting her lips to prepare for the kiss she hoped was coming.

When he felt his control being tested, Lukus finally broke their visual showdown by sweeping his gaze lower to take in his first glimpse of her curvy, naked body.

Christ. Her body is even more perfect than I'd imagined. I was right. She is made for sin.

Her breasts were magnificent. They were big enough to spill over his large hands as he cupped each one, yet firm enough for her tits to stand taut at perfect attention. With an audible groan, Lukus could wait no more. He dove down to latch onto her left nipple with his warm mouth. He attacked her nip with gusto, drawing a matching groan from Tiff. He took his time, sucking and licking her intimately while enjoying the feel of her hands running through his thick, dark hair as she pulled him closer to her chest. He loved that he could hear the fast heartbeat that confirmed his impact on her.

As he moved his mouth to her other nipple, tracing quick kisses across the sensitive valley between her peaks, he noticed she'd begun rocking her body against his in a rhythmic beat, subconsciously broadcasting her desire for him to fill her. He dragged a gasp from her as he allowed his teeth to graze the sensitive tip of her protruding nipple, introducing just the tiniest bit of pain to the pleasure he was delivering.

He was so intoxicated by her that he almost missed her whisper. "Oh yes... that feels so good, Lukus."

With her encouragement, Lukus squeezed her firm breasts tightly in his palms while nipping her harder with his teeth, drawing an almost convulsive shiver.

Only the scent of her liquid heat wafting up between them could drag his attention away from her breasts. It was like an expensive perfume overloading his senses. As nice as her nipples tasted, he knew he wanted more. He *needed* more. A powerful urge to plunge his tongue deep inside her and taste her sweet juice swept through him, and it took all of his well-trained control to maintain the slow, careful pace he'd set. She was like a wild kitten, and he'd need to take his time if he was going to tame her.

Lukus pulled back just enough to study Tiffany's expression. As a Dom, he prided himself in reading subtle cues from a submissive. Still, with all of his experience, he was amazed at just how vulnerable Tiffany made herself in front of him. He could see a storm brewing in her baby blues. It was all on display—her excitement, her lust for him, her vulnerability, and fear of what was coming next. But he could also sense she was up for a challenge; she was ready to let him have it if he went too far.

As he watched, a foreign surge of what he recognized immediately as jealousy flowed through him. Just the thought of anyone else getting close enough to this woman to experience or—God forbid—exploit her precious vulnerability brought out a purely protective instinct he wasn't even sure he'd possessed until that very minute.

He knew how rare the gift of genuine vulnerability was. Lukus was suddenly consumed with the need to claim her as his in the most primal way. Lunging forward, he captured her mouth in a searing, open-mouth kiss. His trademark, disciplined control was eroding as he felt her tongue dueling with his own. He could taste her minty toothpaste as he felt her warm hands sliding up under his T-shirt to stroke his bare, muscular back, pulling him tightly against her own quivering body. He in turn wrapped his arms around her, pulling her against him, and mashing her full breasts into his clothed chest.

In complete harmony, Tiffany lifted his T-shirt as he pulled out of their kiss just long enough to slip it over his head and toss it aside before their bodies snapped back together. The full-frontal, skin-on-skin contact almost unmanned him. As if her aroused nipples weren't enough, Tiff had wrapped her legs around his waist, grinding her warm core against his rock-hard cock as his tongue did to her mouth what his dick was straining to do to her pussy. They spent a long minute passionately groping and kissing before Lukus managed to get a small measure of control back. They might have stopped their kiss, but they remained pressed against each other, foreheads touching, as they each struggled to catch their breath.

Lukus found his voice first, declaring a promise. "You. Me. This is really gonna happen."

Apparently, Tiff was still too affected to form real words. "Uh-huh," was all she could muster.

"Change of plans," he said thickly. "The movie can wait. I'm opting for the bed."

Tiffany broke into a fit of nervous giggles. "I was hoping you might say that."

Lukus chuckled. "So, exactly what'd you have in mind instead, Miss O'Sullivan?" When she remained silent, Lukus gently reached up to cup her face in both hands. "Open up, baby."

Tiffany looked into his eyes and her breath hitched as she recognized his own desire staring back at her.

He chose his words carefully. "I need you to know this. I have *never* wanted to make love to a woman as much as I want to make love to you right this minute, Tiffany. Not fuck. Not screw. Not dominate, but make love. I know it's hard for you to see me as anything other than a Dom, but I need to show you that first and foremost, I'm a man. A man who wants you so very much."

"Oh, Lukus. How do you know exactly what to say? Exactly what I need?" He picked up the slight quaver in her voice.

"I see it in your eyes. I feel it in your kiss, ... the way your body molds to mine. You want it all, just like I do."

"But, you really are still a Dom. I'm not silly enough to think you're going to turn your back on such an important part of who you are."

"Believe me, Tiff. I don't want that, and more importantly, I don't think *you* want me to stop being a Dom either. I know the only reference you have for this lifestyle is watching what that prick, Jake, did to Brianna. But you have to believe me. He. Is. Not. A. Dom. He's a low-life *criminal*—a criminal who belongs in jail for abusing innocent women. Please, let me wipe the slate clean and teach you how special a D/s relationship can be with someone you trust. Do you think you can trust me enough to try?"

It took her a long minute before she whispered her reply. "I do trust you, Lukus. I wouldn't have stayed tonight if I didn't trust you."

Lukus let out a breath of air he hadn't realized he'd been holding. "I promise you, Tiff. All you have to do is say 'no' to anything and I stop. Do you hear me, baby?"

"Yes. But ... well... Are you going to punish me tonight, you know, for not telling you about Jason?"

Lukus didn't miss that she looked almost hopeful he might say yes. It was impossible to hide his smile.

"Let's see how the night goes, shall we? The only thing I know for sure is I'm going to make sweet love to you first. And then..."

Lukus stopped to pull her hard against his body again as he leaned in to whisper his next promise intimately against her ear. "Then I'm going to fuck you over and over, so hard and fast, so long and so deep that you're gonna feel me all day tomorrow." He ended his promise by sucking her earlobe into his warm mouth, nibbling her lightly.

"Oh. My. God."

He could feel her body beginning to tremble and knew they'd done enough talking. Reclaiming her mouth in a passionate kiss, Lukus wrapped his arms tightly around her, dipping his hands lower to grab her bare ass as he effortlessly lifted her body off the barstool. She still had her legs wrapped around his waist, and he could feel her squeezing him tighter, molding herself to him as he turned to head back to his bedroom. When he stopped their kiss to watch where he was walking, Tiffany buried her face into the crook of his neck and began kissing and sucking on the sensitive spot where his neck met his shoulder. Lukus knew she was sucking hard enough to leave a hickey.

That's it, baby. Mark me as your own. I'll give you that much control tonight.

He walked quickly through the darkened great room and down the hall to his master bedroom. Tiffany had left the lights on, threatening to ruin the seductive mood he wanted to set. Lukus flipped the switch, plunging them into darkness. Crossing over to his king-sized bed, he gently laid Tiffany down cross ways, her ass just a few inches in from the edge.

"Don't move. I'm gonna get us a bit of light going. I don't want to miss inspecting every single inch of your beautiful body."

Reaching under his bed, Lukus pulled out a shoebox full of votive candles along with a matchbook he hadn't had the occasion to use in years. He was grateful he'd stowed them under the bed rather than thrown them away as he'd been tempted to do at the time. He took a few minutes to strategically place about a dozen small candles around the room, each one lending a bit more light to the space until he was able to make out Tiffany's lust-filled gaze as she tracked his movements.

Once he had the lighting under control, Lukus crossed to the armoire on the far wall, opening the double doors to reveal a large TV and full entertainment center. With a sly smile to himself, he picked up his eclectically stocked iPod and pulled up one of his rarely used playlists, appropriately labeled "Music to Make Love By." He eyed up the list waiting right above it, labeled "Music to Fuck By."

Now that list has gotten a bit more play and who knows—maybe later. Right now, I think we need something closer to Nora Jones and Babyface.

The soft, sexy sounds of Adele's *Make You Feel My Love* set the mood and, finally satisfied, Lukus came to stand next to the bed to gaze down at Tiffany. She'd pulled her bent legs up to place her feet flat on the edge of the mattress, carefully holding her legs together. Their eyes met briefly before Lukus dropped to his knees next to the bed.

Working to maintain his control, he reached out to hug her bent legs, pulling her body to the very edge before nudging her legs apart. As he opened her wide, it felt like he was opening a Christmas present and the gift was her aromatic, bald pussy, now fully exposed and just inches away.

He wanted so badly to dive in and taste her.

Instead, he turned his head and started by kissing the inside of her left knee before slowly, intimately, nibbling his way down her creamy inner thigh, stopping to occasionally suck her sensitive skin into his mouth, leaving tiny marks on her just as she'd done to his neck minutes before. He could hear her breath catching as he neared the apex between her legs, followed by a disappointed moan when he lifted his mouth and moved to the inside of her right knee to repeat his torturously slow process on the other side of her body. He couldn't help but smile against her soft skin as he heard her little whimpers increasing the closer he got back to her core.

When he finally made it back to her pussy, Tiff had begun to lift her bottom slightly off the bed in hopes of making contact with his warm mouth. Taking the time to both tease and admire her, he finally slipped a single finger through her dripping wet folds, careful not to penetrate her, *yet*. When she could wait no more, Tiff broke her silence. "Oh please, Lukus."

Taking his finger away completely, he teased her. "Please what, Tiff?"

She snapped back quickly. "Oh, please. You know what I want. Please..."

"I don't know. Maybe I'm not reading you right. Maybe I should make you tell me what you want... what you need."

Knowing exactly what Tiff wanted, he didn't

bother waiting for her reply. He lunged forward, dragging his tongue in one long swipe up through her glistening lower lips and ending at her already engorged clit. Tiff lifted her ass up to meet his mouth as he grazed her sensitive nub, desperately seeking more contact. She tasted like sweet honey and for the briefest of moments, Lukus was actually afraid he was going to come in his tight jeans without so much as a single touch to his cock.

Tiffany's primal moans almost undid him. He'd planned on making her wait to come with him inside her, but he could no more tear himself away from the taste of her than she could stop grinding her hips upwards. Sucking her clit fully into his mouth, Lukus plunged two digits deep into her cunt, curling them slightly, in search of her G-spot. Her loud, guttural scream was his first clue he'd successfully found it. His second was her jerking her lower body completely off the bed, thrusting herself up to meet his warm mouth that was still latched onto her sensitive button. He finally replaced his mouth with his thumb so he could look up to admire her as she melted into a mind-blowing climax before his very eyes. A deep feeling of satisfaction washed over him that he was able to bring her such pleasure.

As Tiffany recovered from her orgasm, Lukus stood. Through her post-coital haze, Tiff watched him intently as he reached to unbutton and then unzip his fly. Lukus pushed his jeans down, stepping out and kicking them aside. Tiffany's gaze had left his and was now focused squarely on his crotch as he lowered his briefs to the floor, letting his oversized cock finally hang free.

He'd always known his impressive size played a vital role in both his physical and emotional dominance over subs. For that reason, it'd been a long time since he'd felt nervous with a woman, yet Lukus had to acknowledge he had what could only be described as a few butterflies as he waited for Tiffany's first reaction to seeing him naked. He watched as her initial look of awe was quickly replaced with a lustful, predatory glint.

Hell, yeah. She wants you bad, Sport. You'd better be a good boy and not get overzealous now. We want this to last.

Reaching into the nightstand, he came out with a foil-wrapped condom. Tiffany watched through half-lidded eyes as he rolled the condom onto his long, thick tool. Only when he was done and continued to stand there motionless did she shift her gaze up to meet his. The lust was still glowing, but he saw something deeper—a calm, steady trust shining back at him, and in that moment, he was reminded that without a doubt, what was about to happen was special. Without saying a word, Lukus lifted Tiff to move her into the center of the bed. He slowly crawled in, moving to hover over her as she opened her legs wider. She gasped as she felt the head of his thick cock gently sliding through her wet folds, making sure she was ready for him.

Lukus stayed just inches above her for what seems like an eternity. As anxious as he was to be inside her, he was enjoying watching the expressions flit across Tiffany's face as she breathlessly waited for him. He was caught off guard when she decided to taunt him at this crucial moment.

"I didn't think you were into vanilla, Lukus. Yet, here we are about to make love missionary style on a Saturday night with the lights off."

Damn, I love that sweet sass. I'm going to so enjoy wiping that smile right off her face until she can't think straight.

"Oh baby, this may be vanilla, but I'll be sure to add lots of sprinkles and whipped cream just for you. I can assure you, you're not going to get bored."

Taking control, Lukus started to slowly push his cock into her warm and waiting pussy. He was sure the pace was more torturous for him than for Tiff as he inserted himself into her millimeter by millimeter, savoring each second, never letting his penetrating gaze leave hers as he stretched her wide. The shine in her eyes was ablaze with passion by the time he felt himself fully seated in her tight tunnel. His mind was racing as he fought to maintain control. Holding perfectly still, he let out a deeply held breath. Tiffany threw her arms around his neck, as if she subconsciously wanted to make sure he wasn't going to try to get away from her.

As he pinned her with his stare, he recognized how easy it would be to lose himself completely in her. She was perfection—sin, purity, sass, and submission all rolled into one delectable package. She was like no woman that'd lain down before him. He could see her longing for him etched on her face.

Before he began what he suspected would be his downfall, he pulled her arms away from his neck and took her hands in his, entwining their fingers as closely as their other body parts and stretched her hands above her head, guiding her to a submissive pose. He oh-so-slowly withdrew from her body, and her vulnerable whimper at his retraction edged him closer to losing himself. What he wanted to do was plow her hard and fast, but that would come later. When he'd almost fully withdrawn, he filled her again, slowly.

I'm not gonna last. I can't fucking believe this. I need a distraction. Think about work, about game stats, about how she played like a pro tonight on my court and I'll get to watch her again and again. Shit. This isn't helping... fuuuccckkk.

Once he was in to the base again, Lukus started to pick up the pace, withdrawing again to the tip before ramming back into Tiff's tight folds. The lustful sound she made had him floating in a near out-of-body experience. He pumped in and out of her hot pussy, each stroke harder and faster than the one before and by only the tenth stroke, he was ready to explode inside her.

"Oh, fuck baby, I'm gonna come already... *damn.*"

He'd had every intention of going slow, of making her wait as he made soft, slow love to her luscious body. But when he saw the desire bubbling in her eyes as they were locked with his own, his last control slipped away and Lukus lunged forward, burying his hard cock balls-deep into Tiffany in one final, hard push. She felt so fucking perfect and he wasn't sure what amazed him more —the fact he was shooting his hot cum into the condom with only a few thrusts into her body or the fact that Tiffany's pussy was grasping his cock as she spasmed through her strongest orgasm yet. It took all his strength not to collapse on her as he recovered.

Fuck. What the hell happened? I knew I should have stroked one off in the shower tonight so I would've had a chance in hell of lasting longer.

It was Tiffany's raspy voice that brought him back around. "Oh my God, Lukus. That was amazing. I've never come like that before... *ever.* What the hell did you do?"

Pushing up so he could look down into her eyes, he could see she was absolutely serious.

"I'm glad you enjoyed yourself, baby, but

maybe I should be asking you what *you* did. I've never come so fast like that either... *ever*. I'm so embarrassed."

His heart lurched as she broke into the most adorable smile he'd seen on her yet. "Silly boy. I love that you came so fast. It tells me just how excited you were to be with me. And in case you missed it, I came too."

"Still, I..."

It was Tiff's turn to shush him with her fingers on his lips. "Stop. It was awesome, and in case you forgot, you promised me more tonight and believe me, I'm going to collect on that promise. If you think you're done for the night, you're crazy."

Lukus released a relieved chuckle. "Oh, Tiff, you're so on." He was still buried inside of her as he crushed his mouth down to capture hers in a searing kiss. She was already thrusting her hips up as she felt him quickly growing again, filling her inch-by-inch as the blood flowed to his cock. But Lukus knew he needed to change condoms and reluctantly slid out of her warmth, eliciting a low groan from her. Rolling away and on to his back, he reached down to slide off the spent condom and tie off the end, trapping the cum inside.

They spent a short minute each catching their breath before Lukus pushed to stand next to the bed and dropped the condom in the nearby trashcan.

"I'm gonna go grab us a quick water. Don't

move. I'll be back in just a minute."

"Okay, but don't be gone too long."

Her eyes were shining with a strange mix of emotions Lukus was afraid to interpret and for the briefest of seconds, he felt lightheaded, as if the earth was moving under him. He was nearly knocked on his ass at the unexpected emotions flowing through him as he looked down at Tiffany. He quickly turned, ducking out of the bedroom to head to the kitchen, in part to grab them water, but more importantly, to grab a few minutes to settle his nerves.

Even in his sexual haze, Lukus took the time to recognize how long it'd been since he'd allowed himself to feel this level of intimacy with a woman. While he'd certainly performed any number of very personal, very intimate acts with the submissives he had played with over the years, it was just that—an act. A *game*. Each of them had had their role to play, and each knew it well. Him the aggressor. Her the sexual toy. He knew how to bring pleasure. He knew how to bring pain and he'd delivered both expertly. Until tonight he hadn't recognized the missing ingredient—or more accurately, he hadn't even realized there *was* a missing ingredient that could turn the ordinary into the extraordinary.

I don't know what the hell just happened, but whatever it is, I hope it happens again, and again, and again.

CHAPTER FOUR

TIFFANY

Tiffany was still savoring the afterglow of an orgasm courtesy of what she suspects was the hottest man on the planet. If she had thought she was in danger of getting in over her head earlier in the day, she knew without a doubt now she was already waist deep and sinking fast into the pit of Lukus Mitchell quicksand. She was not sure what scared her more—the fact that he could read her so easily or the fact that she'd loved every minute of their time together.

If this is what being swallowed by quicksand feels like, I'm all in. At least I'll die happy.

But as amazing as that last orgasm had been, Tiff was still not sated, not by a long shot. Lukus's promise for more had her anxiously awaiting his return and feeling almost uneasy about being apart from him. That alone was a big red warning sign for the usually independent Tiffany, who now worked to rebuild her emotional walls of protection.

Earlier in his bathroom, her anxiety had been squarely focused on her fear of the D/s lifestyle and uncertainty over how Lukus may choose to dominate her. Now, just a short time later, that fear had taken a backseat to a much deeper worry; she couldn't shake the undercurrent of a dangerous attraction to him that would surely threaten to undo her when he tossed her aside for his next conquest.

Men like Lukus don't do relationships. Don't let yourself fall too far, Tiff. You're gonna get your heart crushed like a bug on a windshield.

Tiffany didn't have nearly enough time to obsess on that thought before Lukus confidently strode back into the room, carrying a tray with several glasses of ice water and a plate of snacks. He seemed completely comfortable with his nudity, and his powerful, semi-hard erection jutted out from his toned, muscular body. Too late, Tiff wished she'd thought to cover her own nakedness. His hungry gaze on her body did nothing to calm her nerves.

"So, we didn't get to snack on the popcorn I made earlier, but I brought some cheese and crackers along with some grapes just in case you're hungry."

Tiff muttered a quiet "thanks" as she managed to scoot up and sit at the head of the bed, resting her back uncomfortably against the slatted headboard. She hoped she didn't look too obvious as she grabbed Lukus's pillow and casually pulled it into her lap, allowing it to cover as much of her secret wares as she felt she could get away with without looking like a total prude.

It took Lukus about two seconds flat to call her on it.

"Oh no you don't," he quipped, snatching the pillow away. "No getting shy on me now. I haven't even come close to inspecting every inch of your body like I intend to. Now, stretch your legs out for me."

Lukus negotiated the tray across her upper thighs and then moved the pillow to the headboard. "Lean up. That's it."

Tiff had to admit, the pillow cushion behind her felt nice and at least the tray was covering a small portion of her body as Lukus plopped down on the bed next to her. He stretched out on his side just inches away, his head propped up in his left hand. He wasted no time in reaching out with his right to help himself to the snacks and Tiffany was surprised when he diverted his first grape towards her mouth instead of his own.

"Open up for me. Good girl."

Tiff had obediently popped her mouth open

before recognizing his statement for what it was—a gentle command. Before she could give it too much thought, his "good girl" acknowledgement of her immediate compliance caused a rush of pleasure over her newly awakened submissive senses. She was still off balance when Lukus held the glass of water up to her lips and said his next request.

"Drink for me, now. That's it."

It wasn't until Tiff reached out to help herself to a cracker that she realized the real rules of the game. Without a word, Lukus gently took the cracker from her hand and diverted it to her lips. Their eyes met at the moment she opened her mouth to take it from his hand, and the pleasure and approval she saw shining back from his deep green eyes was enough to make her breath catch with her own surprised pleasure.

They spent the next few minutes in an easy companionship listening to Nora Jones, as Lukus fed Tiffany from his hand in between his own bites. Her brain tried to shout to her that she should take offense, to tell him she was a big girl and could feed herself, but for some reason her heart just wouldn't go there. Finally, she refused to ponder the implications too deeply since on some level, it just felt right.

If she still had any doubts, Lukus silently squelched them as he allowed his fingers to follow the last grape into her mouth. Never before had eating been so sensual for Tiff, and his eyes were locked on hers as he slowly began to pull his fingers almost out of her mouth before sliding them back in, a blatant suggestion of what he hoped was soon to come. Tiff couldn't stop the involuntary moan of pleasure from escaping. She was rewarded with Lukus's smile.

I'm in so much trouble here.

Her face must have broadcasted her sudden panic because Lukus quickly sat up and disposed of the food tray on the floor near the door before returning to stand beside the bed, looking down as Tiff waited expectantly for what was to come next. For the first time, Tiff detected what felt like uncertainty rolling off Lukus. Their easy, quiet companionship was quickly charging with renewed sexual tension.

Lukus finally broke their silence. "Now, I believe I made you a promise and it's time I kept it. Up on your knees, baby."

He reached out to pull her forward to kneel in the middle of the bed and pinned her with a predatory glare. "Don't move." There was no ambiguity in his tone. She recognized it for what it was—an order.

Tiff was momentarily confused until she watched him stand and move back to the entertainment center. She was thrilled she had an unfettered view of his naked, athletic body as he moved across the room. Within a minute, the soft sounds of the Commodores's *Easy* was replaced by the hard, sexy beat of AC/DC's *You Shook Me All Night Long*. Surprised by his choice, their eyes met as he walked back towards her. The smile on his face was mischievous.

"It's perfect. This whole playlist is filled with songs just like it. I'm gonna love fucking you hard to the heavy beat, baby."

Tiff's heart did a funny flip-flop. His shameless words were more than invitation. They were a promise, and her body immediately reacted with wild anticipation. Her heart was thumping loudly in her chest. Her breath was becoming labored. She could feel her pussy clenching involuntarily. A desperate longing to feel him inside her washed over Tiff.

As he returned to stand next to the bed, Lukus didn't even pretend to focus on anything other than taking in every nuance of her body. Tiff remained on display on her knees as Lukus feasted on the sight of her, his gaze growing visibly hungrier by the minute. Just when Tiff was about to lose the battle and cover herself, Lukus knelt on the bed, inches away from her now trembling body.

He was close enough for Tiff to not only feel his protruding erection brushing against her tummy, but to also catch a whiff of his masculine Lukus scent mixed with the faint trace of their earlier tryst. She was already close to self-combustion from the memory of Lukus's earlier whispered promise, so the added incentives had the effect of driving her straight into his arms. Like a woman possessed, she threw herself forward, allowing him to capture her mouth and every other damn body part he wanted.

As she reveled in the kiss, she felt Lukus's hard tool sandwiched between their bodies. In that heady moment, her brain was flooded with memories of him on stage dominating Brianna as she had watched, immobile and helpless. She remembered her submissive feelings while tied up in the audience pit, wanting—no, *needing*—Lukus to face-fuck her. She recalled the submissive feelings that had coursed through her body as she had touched each of the sex toys in his bathroom, the vision of Markus dominating Brianna onstage as he'd pounded her relentlessly until they'd both screamed out in their joint climax. The memories were all there in that one moment, raining down on Tiff.

In one swift motion, Lukus moved them horizontally, their heads at the head of the bed, his muscular body pressing her into the mattress. Before she could catch her breath, he'd captured her hands and lifted them above her head, loosely holding them there as they tried to catch their breath. In a moment of weakness, Tiff tested his hold and recognized she could easily get away from him, if she wanted to. Just that knowledge calmed her enough to enjoy the feel of his hard cock as it grinded into her upper thigh. With a wolfish grin,

Lukus finally let her in on his wanton plans for her.

"I seem to remember you wanting to stay down on the stage tonight to re-enact the little scene Markus and Brianna put on. I may not have wanted to take you for the first time on the dirty floor of the stage, but nothing's going to stop me from taking you in exactly the same way right here in my bed. I'm going to fuck you like you've never been fucked before. I'm gonna fuck you like you deserve, Tiff."

His naughty words were like a key opening up some secret submissive closet deep inside her. A warm glow spilled out, seeping into every pore of her body, centering at the apex between her legs. Like a woman crazed, she began to thrust her hips up, trying to take him inside her, suddenly desperate for him to dominate her.

With a slight chuckle, Lukus chided her. "Patience now. I want you to hold onto the slates of the headboard. You're not going to let go. I don't want to tie you down, not yet. You think you can hold on?"

Tiff heard him. She even understood him, but found the formation of words at this crucial moment impossible.

Lukus seemed worried. "Are you okay? Do you need me to stop?"

The threat of his stopping finally jarred the words right out of her.

"Oh my God, no! Don't stop!"

This time Lukus couldn't help but chuckle. "Well, okay then. I'll take that as a 'yes.' You'll be able to hold on while I take you hard?"

"Oh, Lukus, I think so. I hope so." She didn't sound very convincing, not even to herself.

"Well, I hope so, too. I'd hate to have to add on more punishments for letting go."

The twinkle in his eye told Tiff he was only teasing. Still, she was worried she wouldn't be able to hold on and there was a minuscule part of her that actually *wanted* him to tie her down like he had done down in the audience pit. If only she had known how to formulate the words to ask him. Even in her precarious state, she recognized the similarities between how Brianna couldn't share her own submissive needs with Markus, and how she couldn't share her needs with Lukus. It gave her a better understanding of what her friend had been through.

Lukus was wearing a curious new smile she'd never seen on him before.

"You want me to tie you down, don't you?"

When she didn't answer, he took her chin in his hand and squeezed, not very hard, but hard enough to know he expected her full attention.

"I can see we're going to have to lay down a few more ground rules already tonight. When I ask you if you want something, I need you to answer me, and not with the answer you think I want to hear, but the truth. Starting from day one, there'll be no secrets between us. Nothing is off limits to discuss. There'll be no boundaries we won't eventually test, but we can only do that if we talk to each other. I'll be damned if I'm going to let us make the same fucking mistake Markus and Brianna did. Do you understand me?"

She swallowed nervously. How could he have known what she'd been thinking? When she didn't formulate an answer fast enough, Lukus squeezed the slightest bit, effectively recapturing her attention.

"Answer me. Do you understand, Tiff?"

"Yes, Lukus. I understand." It came out as a whisper, but he heard.

"Excellent. Now, would you trust me enough to let me tie you down tonight, baby?"

The words he used had changed ever so subtly, but they made all the difference to her.

"Oh yes, Sir. I do trust you."

The look on his face as her answer registered was amazing. She could hear pure joy in his reply.

"That's my *very*, good girl."

Her heart did a flip-flop at the thought of being *his* anything. Lukus didn't even try to hide his pleasure with the surprising turn of events. He left the bed and rushed to the bathroom, returning quickly with the very same fleece-lined cuffs Tiffany had held just a short hour ago—the very cuffs she'd acknowledged she wanted to try with

Lukus. Little had she known she'd get her chance so soon.

Lukus knelt on the bed next to her. The soft restraints felt luxurious against her skin as he secured them around her wrists. While Lukus focused on getting her arms stretched upwards to the headboard, Tiffany fixated on his hard cock swinging just inches away from her face as he knelt next to her. When he leaned forward to lock her wrists to the headboard with a carabiner attached to the cuffs' D-rings, Tiffany closed the final inch between them and sucked the head of his cock into her warm mouth. She'd known he was big, but she was surprised to feel how wide she needed to open just to take in the first few inches of his semi-hard manhood.

Pulling away, Lukus admonished her. "Oh fuck, baby. You need to stop now. It feels amazing, but I want to come inside you."

Tiffany didn't bother hiding her disappointment. "Coming in my mouth *is* inside me. I want to taste you, Lukus. You got to taste me."

He looked conflicted and Tiff suspected he wasn't used to women who acted this aggressively in bed. As a Dom, she knew he was used to calling all the shots, but just like he got to lay down some of his rules with her on day one, she knew she needed to lay down a few of her own—one of which was that as submissive as she might end up being, she would never be a 24/7 sub who blindly followed orders. They'd need to plan a discussion on finding the right balance.

"That I did, and you taste amazing. I promise, I plan on you tasting me often, but right now, I need to get inside you.

Hearing his urgency, she decided to let it go for now.

Tiff could see his hunger for her reflected in his eyes as he lifted first one ankle to secure it in a fleece-lined cuff before moving to her other side. He pulled the buckle snug on each restraint to make sure she wasn't going to be in pain, even though she suspected he was devilishly looking forward to her being at his complete mercy.

Once both restraints were secured, Lukus lifted her legs off the bed, pushing them back over her body and spreading them wide. She could see a carabineer attached to each cuff that he quickly clipped to two different rails of the headboard, ensuring she was now held captive and at his mercy.

She'd never been splayed open in this position before and the added vulnerability of her limbs being tied down pushed her into a submissive mindset she hadn't even known was possible. It was one thing to read about something in a book, to watch it on TV, or in a movie, or to even see it live on a stage in a club. Not until this very moment did Tiffany realize just how different it was to be a participant instead of just a voyeur. So far, she really liked the upgrade.

Once she was secured, Lukus reached to grab a condom and quickly slid it onto his already steeled erection, before moving to the center of the bed. Tiff was glad when he took the time to place a pillow under her head. Not only was it more comfortable, but it lifted her head to give her a better view of what was about to happen to the rest of her body.

Tiffany's heart was racing like never before. She could hear the pounding of her heart in her ears and felt a sudden release of wetness between her legs as her still empty pussy clenched expectantly, preparing for what she knew was coming. Lukus took his time, devouring every inch of her body with his eyes and his hands.

Unlike Markus who plunged into Bri immediately, Lukus dragged it out by caressing her inner thighs, tweaking her nipples, and seductively massaging her ass, carefully avoiding touching the body parts she was dying for him to accost. He effectively ratcheted up their desire until they were both breathing so hard Tiff felt like she could hyperventilate. She was forced to finally beg.

"Please..."

A devilish smile crossed his lips. "Please... what?" She knew then he'd been waiting for her.

"Please... I need you."

"You have me. I'm right here." To prove his

point, Lukus drew a finger lightly through her wet folds, barely grazing her sensitive clit, but forcing Tiff to buck her hips up as best she could in an attempt to maintain contact with him. His chuckle proved he was having fun teasing her.

"Lukus..."

"Tiffany..."

This time, he dragged his finger through her lower lips going deeper and lingering on her clit long enough to draw a pleasurable moan from her before removing his digit.

"Oh God. You're torturing me. Please..."

"Maybe now is when I should torment you into telling me all your secrets. Let's start with how you learned to play basketball like Michael Jordan?"

"LUKUS! Now is not the time to be talking about basketball!"

Damn him for remaining completely calm as he tweaked her vulnerable nipples again.

"I think now is the perfect time to talk about basketball."

She could see the mischief playing in his beautiful green eyes.

"Lukus Mitchell, don't you make me regret letting you tie me down."

"Tsk, tsk, tsk. So sassy. So, if you don't want to talk about basketball, what *do* you want to do?"

This time, he allowed his fingers to slide through the wet folds of her pussy, dipping inside just long enough to give her hope he might finger fuck her to another climax.

Knowing he'd be able to wait her out, she finally gave in and begged. "You need to fuck me now, Lukus. Please, fuck me hard like you promised me you would."

She watched as all playfulness left him. It was as if he'd been waiting for her to supply the secret password.

"That's it, baby. I wanted to hear you ask for it. God, you're so beautiful, Tiffany. I'm gonna fuck you just like I promised—long and hard, fast and deep."

With their eyes locked, Lukus lined up his erection and in one fluid thrust, buried himself as deep in Tiffany as he could go, surely hitting places no one else had ever touched before. The feel of him filling her so completely was amazing, but it was the sound of his crying out her name in ecstasy that thrilled Tiffany the most.

She thought she'd been prepared—she really had. But nothing could have prepared Tiff for the overwhelming pleasure consuming her body as Lukus set a hard and fast pace, pulling his rock-hard cock out again and again, only to plunge it in faster and deeper with each thrust. She wasn't exactly sure how he did it, but it was like he was rocking his body as he thrusted in a manner that brought him in contact not only with her engorged clit, but also with her secret spot deep inside of her.

It only took a short minute for her first orgasm to start. It hit her so hard it was like a truck rolling over her, the pleasure so intense she felt as if she was exploding into a million pieces. Even as she started to recover from one orgasm, another exploded, this one drawing out a long guttural rant Tiff couldn't stop if she had had to.

"Oh, my God, yes! Oh, Lukus! Don't stop honey! That's it! Thank you! Fuck me! Fuck me hard! Oh Jesus! I'm coming again! Fuck... yes... more... more! Oh, shit! I'm coming again, honey... "

At some point, through her orgasmic haze, Tiffany felt Lukus moving from his kneeling position to stretch out and place his face only inches from her own. He'd slowed his pace slightly, taking more time to slowly draw out of her body only to thrust forward again and again.

Stroking her hair gently, he coaxed her. "Baby, open up. I want to see your eyes when you come with me. I'm so close."

When Tiff opened her eyes, the sight of him knocked the wind out of her. He was beautiful, magnificent really. And right this minute, he was all hers. Vulnerability crashed over her, not because of the hot sex, but because of the power this man had over not only her body, but her heart. She watched as the pleasure they were sharing washed over him and felt privileged to see him melt into a powerful orgasm that had him screaming her name.

"Oh Tiffany, baby. Damn, you're so fucking tight! Yesssss!"

The feel of his powerful contractions pushed Tiffany into her final orgasm. This time, instead of a rant of dirty talk, she found herself fighting back tears— tears of joy, pleasure, and sexual relief. She managed to hold them down to a few stray drops until Lukus lowered himself fully on top of her and began to suck intimately on her neck while remaining buried deep inside of her. Their bodies connected perfectly, like locking puzzle pieces and for some strange reason, this final act of intimacy unleashed a floodgate of tears. Before she knew it, she was sobbing.

That's it, Tiff. Nothing like ruining one of the best moments of your life. Keep it up. He's going to think you've lost it.

Through her tears she saw his confusion. Thinking he might have hurt her, Lukus quickly extracted his deflating cock from her pussy and rushed to bring her legs down to the bed. He untied her arms, massaging them as he knelt next to her.

"Tiff, talk to me, baby. What's wrong? Did I hurt you?"

For some strange reason, the concern in his voice only pushed Tiff to cry that much harder. Even as she was doing it, she knew how irrational her reaction was, but try as she might, she just couldn't stop crying for several long minutes. It was like Lukus's powerful claiming of her body had broken a dam she wasn't even aware she'd constructed. The dam had clearly been holding back emotions she had successfully hidden away, even from herself.

Tiffany felt more exposed than ever as she let her fears, vulnerability, and desire to submit cave in on her. The dam had kept her strong and independent and ready to tackle the world alone. Without it, she felt needy, and needing a man like Lukus Mitchell was dangerous.

Lukus finally lay next to her and pulled her into his arms, letting her snuggle up next to him while he held her through her mini meltdown, quietly trying to calm her as she cried into his bare chest.

When she was finally down to sniffles, Lukus sat up and first removed and disposed of his condom before reaching for a box of tissues. He laid Tiff onto her back and hovered over her, gently wiping away her tears. He held a fresh tissue to her nose.

"Blow for me."

When he had her cleaned up and calmed down, he lay next to her on his side, reaching out to cup her face in his hand. "Are you ready to talk about it?"

"No," she mumbled.

Tiff was only now starting to figure out what had been at the real root of her crying jag and she had absolutely no intention of sharing her hypothesis with Lukus. She'd already given him way too much power over her considering they'd only known each other for twelve hours.

"You know I'm not gonna let this drop, right?"

"You need to, Lukus. I'm fine."

"Maybe. Maybe not. Let me be the judge of that."

Tiff tried valiantly to rebuild a portion of her protective dam. "I think I can judge for myself if I'm fine or not." Her answer came out sharper than she'd intended.

In a flash, Lukus was straddling her waist and had her lifted into a sitting position, trapping her while bringing her face to within inches of his own.

"Tiffany Lauren O'Sullivan, this behavior will not be tolerated. That was, without a doubt, one of the most amazing sexual experiences of my life, and believe me, that's saying something. I'll be damned if I'm about to let you ruin it by sobbing for five minutes as if it was one of the *worst* experiences in *your* life and then watch you clam up and refuse to talk about it. Now, what the hell happened? I thought you were there with me. I thought it was special for you too."

She could hear a fear and vulnerability in his tone that was so unexpected and knew with a certainty he was never going to let it drop. Did she try to make something up or did she follow the rule he had set out not so long ago—a rule to always tell the truth?

"Just spit it out Tiff. I'm a big boy. I can take it." His words had a sharp edge to them.

He was pulling away from her. She felt it. Maybe not physically, but emotionally. She knew now her silence was causing him to think he had somehow hurt her, or worse, that he hadn't satisfied her.

I'm right back to the same two choices. I can put on my dress and drive away, never to see him again and always wonder what could have been, or I can dive into the deep end of the pool and hope he'll catch me.

Looking into his deep green eyes, she knew she only had one choice after all. Leaving was not an option. "It's just... well..."

The damn waterworks were starting again, but this time Lukus stayed in place, watching her patiently.

"Please Tiff. I really need to know what I did."

"Oh Lukus, don't you see? You ruined me!" She blurted.

"I hurt you?"

Through her tears, Tiff repeated. "No, you *ruined* me."

Lukus was totally confused. "I don't understand."

As she panicked, Tiff's tears were coming harder until her final answer came out in a sobbing whoosh. "You ruined me! It was so perfect! How is any man ever going to be able to satisfy me ever again? When you get tired of me, I'm going to have to go out there and find some other poor schmuck who's going to have to try to come after you and let's face it—they're never gonna measure up, because Jesus Fucking Christ, you gave me like a dozen orgasms and... well... you ruined me!"

Lukus couldn't help himself. With a visible rush of relief, he burst out laughing.

Laughing? I spill my inner most thoughts and the jerk is laughing at me?

Tiff watched as he tried his best to get his laughter under control before he reached for more tissues to comfort her

"Oh baby. You scared me there for a few minutes. I promise you. You don't have anything to worry about. Now blow again for me." Holding another tissue up to her nose, Lukus helped calm Tiffany down for the second time.

When she was finally collected, she worked up the courage to confront him. "I can't believe you laughed at me, Lukus. I'm not joking."

Taking her face in both hands, Lukus looked deep into her eyes as he answered. "I'm not joking either, Tiff. You have nothing to worry about."

"Easy for you to say."

"Yes, it is since I'll fucking castrate the first guy who tries to put his hands on you, baby. I have absolutely no idea how it happened, but you've ruined me too, Tiff. So let me be clear. We have a lot to get to know about each other and as we do, I may find myself willing to bend on some things, like letting you take the brownies with the hard edges." He grinned at her knowingly before continuing on. "But one thing I will *not* bend on is that no other poor bastard needs to worry about satisfying you because until further notice, that job belongs to me, and me alone. Do you hear me?"

Tiffany shook her head. "This is crazy. It's too fast."

"It's fast, yes. So, if we need to slow it down, we can. But, fast or slow, it doesn't change the fact that this body is off limits to anyone else but me." He hugged her closer to make his point.

Her first reaction was to jump for joy, but then it hit her. Pulling back, she reached out to poke him in the chest, confronting him.

"And what about this body, Lukus? Is this body off limits to anyone but me?"

He fixed her with that hot coals smile. "Absolutely... on one condition, that is."

She was so surprised at this turn of events she could barely get a squeak out. "And what condition is that?"

Lukus leaned in so close she could feel his warm breath. "You have to promise to keep calling me 'honey' when you're coming. *Fuck*, that rant was hot, baby."

It was Tiffany's turn to laugh at Lukus. "Oh honey, I don't think that'll be a problem."

He was so close she could feel his growing

erection poking her, clearly looking for some attention. Without missing a beat, Lukus had them horizontal once again as he crushed her body beneath him, claiming her mouth with his own, his tongue demanding entry.

Wow, it looks like he really meant his promise. I think I could get used to swimming in the deep end.

CHAPTER FIVE

TIFFANY

Tiffany's muscles were screaming for release. The constant strain of trying to escape from the ropes binding her body to the padded table where she was sprawled, facedown, was taking its toll on her limbs. Her scream was muffled by an overly large ball-gag.

She was facing away from her captor, so she could only feel him slowly massaging her lower back, his hand moving downward to stroke her ass almost lovingly. Her earlier panic subsided as she allowed the tenderness of his caress to lull her into calm. His hand drifted lower to stroke her wet labia splayed open between spread-eagled legs tied to the far edges of the wide table. The agile fingers flicked across her clit just long enough to draw a moan from deep within before diving in and out of her pussy several times, drawing out the gathering wetness.

She was so focused on the probing fingers bringing her pleasure that she was completely unprepared for the searing pain of the punishingly strong cane stroke as it struck her squarely across both ass cheeks, spreading fire equally to both rounded globes. She only had a second to recover from the heat spreading through her ass before the feel of the next lash connected squarely with the lower portion of her butt, forcing a long scream.

The scorching pain was bad enough, but it was the chilling chuckle of her punisher that made her blood run cold. She could hear the joy in his sadistic laughter as he continued to punish her naked body with strokes from the thick cane on her defenseless ass. She felt the dreaded shame of losing control pushing to the fore of her thoughts as she allowed her panic to consume her.

Using every ounce of strength she could muster, she struggled to free her arms or legs from their hold, managing only to dig the restraints deeper where rough rope met tender skin. It was when the cane connected with her bare back that she finally heard her own scream breaking through her fragile dreamlike state.

She felt his warm hands on her upper arms, gently shaking her, before reality slowly started to seep into her consciousness. It was his masculine scent that came next, helping to slow her racing heart. But it wasn't until she heard his voice that she realized what had truly happened.

"Tiffany. Wake up, baby. You're having a nightmare."

Lukus's voice was reassuringly strong, allowing Tiffany's dark dream to slowly slink back into the recesses of her mind where, no doubt, it would come out to torture her again. Her eyes fluttered open, seeking the comforting reassurance of Lukus's protection from a dream that had haunted her for what seemed like forever. Her breathing was labored as she tried to calm down.

Lukus pinned her ocean-blue eyes with a probing glare, seeking to ascertain if she was okay. In the dim pre-dawn light, Tiff could see the concern etched on his face. She tried to pass off a reassuring smile, but she was pretty sure her shivering gave away her mental status. She tried to keep the quaver out of her voice as she replied. "I'll be okay in a minute, Lukus. I just need to wake up a bit and then I'll be fine."

"You're not fine. You were actually screaming as if you were hurt. What the hell were you dreaming about?"

Lukus had rolled her onto her back and was hovering over her, blanketing her as if he meant to stand between her and anything that dared threaten her. Tiff couldn't resist reaching up to stroke his stubble-covered face, taking comfort in feeling he was real and not just a figment of her imagination.

My own Prince Charming, intent on coming to my rescue.

His watchful concern was touching and made Tiff's heart flutter. He was being so protective of her, even against her imaginary demons. Still, she had no intention of discussing her recurring nightmare, at least not tonight, and not with Lukus. There was nothing he could do about it, and the details were just too intimate and embarrassing.

She couldn't help but question why the dream would resurface tonight, but realized the answer was obvious. It was no coincidence the dream, which had been gratefully dormant for over a year, chose tonight to rear its ugly head. Her face must have portrayed her epiphany.

"What is it? Talk to me."

Lukus stroked her hair, carefully swiping the sweat-dampened locks away from her face, removing the last small veil she had to hide behind. He didn't have to say another word. His last command was hanging in the air. She knew he expected answers.

Damn him. He knows it's important. I don't know how, but he knows.

Tiff fell back on her first line of defense. She snapped her eyes closed, trying to hide her disorganized emotions from Lukus long enough to formulate a truthful answer which would both appease him and would still protect herself from the pain of delving too deep into her demons. It was bad enough they crept up and impacted her sleep. She'd be damned if she was going to let them start to infiltrate her waking hours as well.

"Open up, Tiff. You can't just close your eyes every time you don't want to talk to me."

Keeping her eyes closed, she replied. "Of course, I can." She let a playful smile creep to her face, hoping her sassy response would distract him from his original mission.

"I'll rephrase. You *won't* close your eyes every time you don't want to talk to me. Open."

Tiff wanted to be angry at his tone... at his expectation he could demand and she would just obey. But now that her protective dam had fallen, she found a welcome, warm burn igniting deep within as she realized that for the first time, she'd met a man who wasn't going to let her roll right over him. The realization was both frightening and strangely exciting. She finally took a deep breath and opened her eyes to see he'd moved even closer; his handsome face hovering just inches away.

"That's my girl." His possessive words mingled with his intensely dominant gaze to make her feel as if she'd just been encased by his protective shield... as if nothing was ever going to hurt her again. It felt damn good.

"Now baby, I think I've made my point clear, but just in case you missed it, we're not going to follow in Markus and Brianna's footsteps and avoid talking about topics that may feel uncomfortable.

Be warned. Just like down on the stage last night, I didn't try to hide anything from you. I took a chance by telling you the truth, knowing it might hurt you. I did it because it was the right thing to do. I've never been one to play games. That means we may end up having to say things to each other that might hurt or feel embarrassing, but I don't give a shit. I can't fix things I don't know about."

"Lukus, I get it. But truly... there's nothing for you to fix. It's just a dream I have sometimes...."

Before Tiff could finish her sentence, he interrupted. "So, you've had it before?"

"Yes, but..."

"And is someone hurting you?"

"Yes, but..."

"Sexually?"

Tiff was tired of him cutting her off. She was also aware he was quickly homing in on the root of her nightmare. "Lukus, please. Let it go."

The standoff had begun. He held, waiting for her response. She refused to answer and had to work hard to keep her eyes open as she watched the emotions flit across Lukus's face in the dim lighting. She could see his determination. They were suddenly playing a game of chicken. Who would flinch first? The long, silent seconds dragged on like hours.

Damn... he's good at this.

"Fine. It's a nightmare I've had on and off for the last few years. I honestly haven't had it in so long I'd hoped it was gone for good. Apparently, I was wrong."

"Who's in it? Who's hurting you?"

She knew the truth was going to set off fireworks, yet he was the one who laid down the rules. Tiff got a small feeling of hollow victory at the thought of answering him truthfully.

Serves his ass right for pushing me to talk about it.

She didn't expound. She didn't need to. One word would do. "Jake."

She didn't miss the sharp intake of his breath as he internalized her answer. If possible, his deep green eyes turned black in the dim light. She got the impression he was working hard to maintain his temper before quietly replying. "I thought he'd only hurt Brianna. I didn't know he'd touched you, too. Tell me every single thing that prick did to you, baby."

Tiff was acutely aware that for the first time, she was talking about Jake's abuse to a man who not only actually gave a shit about how fucked up both she and Brianna were over Jake's abuse, but she was talking to a man who was more than prepared to actually *do something* about it. That realization was both exhilarating and frightening. As much as she'd love for Jake to pay for all he'd done to terrorize them, she didn't want Lukus to do anything stupid that'd get him in trouble... or worse... hurt.

"Lukus, please. It's in the past. Let it go."

"The hell it's in the past. You had the dream tonight. Lying in *my* bed... in *my* arms." His calm was eroding. She felt the hurricane brewing behind his response. "Markus and I are gonna deal with the bastard. Now, tell me *exactly* what he's done to you. Don't leave anything out, do you hear me?"

"Lukus, believe me. I want to see Jake pay for all the pain he's caused, but I don't want you to do anything stupid. Please..."

"I'm not gonna do anything stupid. I just need facts."

"Well, the fact is he never really touched me... not physically, anyway. Sometimes I think it might have been easier if he had."

Tiff felt his grip on her upper arm constricting as he replied. "I don't want to hear you ever say that again, Tiff. I've heard firsthand what he's done to Brianna so I don't ever want you to wish that for yourself."

"You're right. I'm sorry. I just get mad at myself for letting him scare me so much. He loved to torture Bri both physically and mentally. He just took joy in torturing me emotionally."

"I need specifics. What did he do *exactly*?"

Tiff knew Lukus was trying to help, but his pushing was making things worse. She felt like a spineless dishrag when more hot tears burned her eyes. She'd already cried more times in front of this man than she had in the last six months together. She didn't like playing the role of the damsel in distress, but taking another look into Lukus's dark eyes, she could see he was not going to back down.

With a deep sigh, Tiff plunged into the story. "He never touched me. In the beginning, he tried hard to hide what he was doing to Brianna. Eventually, though, he knew I was trying to get her to leave him. I didn't like the changes I was seeing in her. I knew he was abusing her. One night, when he brought her home with a big bruise across her cheek and... she was unable to sit down, I made the mistake of screaming at him to get out and never call her again. I threatened if he didn't leave her alone, I was going to call my brothers and tell them what he was doing to Bri and he'd be sorry. He knew most of my brothers were cops and I thought he'd be too afraid of getting them on his case. Little did I know, he'd figure out I was bluffing and actually use it against me."

"What do you mean, you were bluffing? You damn well should've asked them for help."

"You have no idea how much I wish I would've, but at the time I was too ashamed to go to them and Jake knew it."

"Ashamed of what? That you knew he was abusing Bri?"

"No... it's just... well." He was patiently waiting for her to finish. "You won't understand."

"The hell I won't."

"We barely know each other, Lukus. You have

no idea about my childhood... my family life, just like I have no idea about yours."

"I don't need to know about your family life, Tiff. I know this. If you'd gone to one of your brothers with this story, cop or no cop, they would've damn well helped you take care of the problem."

"Exactly."

"So..."

"So, I couldn't let them get in trouble. I knew how protective they are of Bri and me. She'd been home with me dozens of times through our college years. They love her like a sister. Jake would've ended up in a shallow grave somewhere and they'd have ended up kicked off the force... in jail."

"Not if they're even half as smart as you are, baby." Lukus's sly grin told Tiff she had been right to worry about telling him the story.

"Believe me, I hate him so much, I entertained the idea a few times myself, but it's not that simple. Jake is... well, he's... devious." She took a break in hopes he'd let it drop. His probing glare was unwavering. He would hear the story.

Tiff continued on, the defeat evident in her voice. "He recorded a tape. He showed it to me once... you now... to make sure I knew he was telling the truth. It had him outlining how Brianna was his willing sub and he was her Dom. In it, he made sure to talk about many of the depraved things he did to her, but he said how much she loved the submission and the pain... that she actually got off on it." Her voice took on a wicked edge as she continued. "The bastard even recorded several sessions where she was enjoying... well... you know how she is." Tiff could feel herself blushing as she took a short break to make sure Lukus was with her. She prayed he didn't ask her for the gory details of how the tape showed Brianna coming while being strapped and spanked to bruising with a heavy wooden paddle.

Thankfully, Lukus seemed to have a good handle on Brianna's particular pain tolerance as he nodded her to continue. "Of course, he never included the true abuse on the tape. The things he was doing to her without her consent—that she *didn't* enjoy. That was bad enough, but the worst part of the tape was when he went on to say he felt threatened and harassed by my family of cops and if anything should ever happen to him, the police should investigate them as they would most likely be responsible. He had a copy of the tape left sealed at his lawyer's office to be opened in the event of his death."

"That fucker. He knew you'd never want to risk getting your brothers involved."

"Exactly. Once he had me backed into the corner, his gloves came off. He went out of his way to make sure I knew every sick detail he was doing to Bri because he'd made sure I'd be too afraid to stop him. I got to the point where I would've gladly risked getting myself in trouble, but never my brothers. The bastard called me that Valentine's weekend when he was on the way back with Brianna beaten and bleeding. He took joy in making sure I'd be home to witness his handiwork firsthand. Thankfully, Bri had finally had enough and I thought we'd finally seen the last of him. But even after Bri finally got away from him, I still lived in fear some other woman he was terrorizing would finally have enough and take him out and it would still drag my poor brothers into this mess."

Tiff tried to decide if she should stop there or finish the story. She could see he was waiting, as if he knew there was more. "It's why I'm so furious with Brianna for letting him back in her life again. Not only am I afraid he could truly kill her one day if he isn't stopped... but... well, she doesn't know this. I'd just about decided to ask Markus to help me get the tape back legally. I know Bri told him about Jake right after they met and I suspected he'd want to get even with Jake as much as I did. Then she had to go and let the asshole fuck her again, and his new round of blackmail started, and I knew then I could never go to Markus for help. Not anymore."

"Oh Tiff, come here, baby." Lukus rolled to his back, pulling Tiff to snuggle up against him, safely cocooned in his protective arms. She tried hard not to dissolve into the threatening tears yet again. She wanted to be strong, but the weight of her nightmare combined with the relief of finally being able to share the burden of her guilty feelings for putting her brothers in danger made it impossible to hold back her tears. For what seemed like the tenth time since meeting Lukus, Tiffany found herself crying against his strong chest. For once, she felt the tears were justified.

Several minutes passed. He didn't try to tell her she was silly. He didn't try to stop her tears. It was exactly what she needed. When she was finally calm, he hugged her to him tightly, still stroking her back gently, but she wasn't fooled. She knew his mind had been racing with all the possibilities he had available to deal with Jake. Before she could warn him off getting involved, he was already pressing for more information. "So, what exactly does he do to you in the nightmare?"

"Please..."

"Tiffany." His voice was firm.

"Fine." Her unguarded response came out like a petulant child's sass to a demanding parent. She was happy she no longer had to look him in the eye as she described her reoccurring dream. "I keep dreaming it's me he's torturing in the video. That it's me, instead of Bri, he has tied down and immobile. That it's me he's beating with the cane over and over. When I'm lucky, I wake up before it gets to the point where I start bleeding. When I'm really unlucky, I keep dreaming long enough where I see my brothers breaking in to shoot him dead.

Then they start to untie me and I can see the disappointment in me reflected in their eyes. They're disgusted I was mixed up in the BDSM lifestyle. They treat me like I'm a whore and tell me I deserved what I got."

"You know that's completely irrational, right?"

"Maybe... maybe not. I'm the youngest daughter in a very Catholic family. Let's just say I'm pretty sure my father thinks I'm still a virgin. I know my brothers are a bit more realistic, but they'd never approve of... well... of..."

"Of me."

"I didn't say that."

"You don't need to. I can just imagine what it's gonna be like taking me home to meet the parents. 'Mom... Dad... I'd like you to meet my boyfriend, Lukus. He owns a sex club where he's the Master in charge of delivering punishments to naughty submissives.' I'm sure they'll welcome me with open arms." Tiff could hear the bitterness in his voice and it made her panic he was going to decide a relationship with her was going to be too much trouble after all.

"Well, I haven't given it much thought, but I admit I'd more likely introduce you as owning a security firm. Considering my dad is a retired cop and my brothers are either lawyers or cops, I'm pretty sure they'd welcome you with open arms as a fellow law enforcement official."

"So, you want to hide the truth."

"No. You do own a security firm. That's the truth."

"But you'd want to hide the fact that I'm a Dom?"

"Is that a trick question? Of course, I'd want to hide that fact. They'll have trouble thinking I'm making out with someone, let alone having sex... kinky sex at that. If they knew I used to go to BDSM clubs and what kind of books I read... well, let's just say they wouldn't be happy. They're very traditional."

"How old are you, Tiff?"

"What difference does that make? Anyway, don't you know it's not polite to ask a woman how old she is?"

"I'm not asking any woman. I'm asking you, the woman I want to protect and spend time with. The woman I'm lying in bed with after having fucked her senseless—more than once, I might add. Seems like a pretty simple question."

"Well, when you put it that way. I'm twenty-seven, almost twenty-eight."

"So, you actually think your parents believe you've stayed a virgin at the age of twenty-seven? They do know what you look like, right? How amazing and beautiful and smart you are?"

"Thanks, but I'm still their little girl."

"Well, then, they're gonna be in for a bit of a surprise when you take me home, aren't they? There's no fucking way anyone is gonna be in a room with us for more than three minutes and not figure out we want to fuck each other's brains out at the next possible opportunity."

Tiff giggled at the image and decided to tease him. "And who said I was going to ever take you home to meet them?"

"Oh, I'll meet 'em, Tiff. You can count on that."

Tiff's heart raced at the implications of his words. He was making it crystal clear this wasn't just a one-night stand. He was backing up his earlier declaration that she belonged with him, and that they were going to see where this attraction they were sharing was going to take them. A warm glow flowed through her at the thought of spending more time with Lukus, both in and out of the bedroom.

They spent a few minutes in silence. She might have thought Lukus was going back to sleep if it were it not for the gentle caress he maintained from her shoulder, tracing down her bare arm and back up again. It was soothing and intimate and she was getting drowsy by the time he spoke softly.

"I know we haven't really talked about the details of what the D/s lifestyle means to each of us yet, and there's plenty of time for us to figure it out, but I want to let you know I'm putting canes on your hard limit list, baby. I promise you right now. I'll never use a cane on you. After learning more about Jake's methods, I regret using one on Brianna earlier, and I don't want you to have to worry about it ever happening to you. I won't put you through that."

Lukus's unexpected pronouncement hit her hard for many reasons, not the least of which was that he was so perceptive not only to how afraid she was of pain in general, but canes specifically. She fought to keep her emotions under control and managed to squeak out, "Thank you, Lukus. You have no idea how much that means to me."

Before she knew it, Lukus had her flipped onto her back and he was trapping her beneath him. She could feel his growing erection grinding against her upper thigh and knew he was getting ready to make good on his earlier promise to make sure she felt him all day. He caught her off guard. "Enough of this heavy shit. Let's play a little game."

"Okay. What kind of a game?" Based on the predatory glint in his eyes, Tiff was pretty sure he wasn't about to suggest a board game.

"It's a continuation of the game we started in the kitchen yesterday. A bit of truth-or-dare—a way for us to get to know more about each other. Like hard limits, turn-ons and offs." Before Tiff even agreed he shot out his first question. "So, tell me, baby. What's your favorite kind of punishment? We'll leave canes on the *no* list, but I'd like to know what's on the *yes* list."

Tiffany blurted out the first thing that came to her mind. "I thought you said we'd had enough of the heavy shit. That's a heavy question, Lukus."

"No, it's not. If I asked for a complete and total inventory, that would be heavy. Just give me one thing you've enjoyed."

He had to see the panic in her eyes as she tried to formulate her answer.

Great. Now is when I get to confess my entire BDSM experience is as a voyeur and despite my deep dark desires, I've never had so much as a decent over-the-knee spanking. Isn't he in for a surprise when he finds out the Master's Master picked the complete and utter novice out of the line-up of all possible playmates? He's sure to get bored with me in less than a week.

"What's the matter? Did I say something wrong?"

"No... it's just... well..." Tiffany took a deep breath and plunged forward with the most truthful answer she could give. "Not counting reading books and watching from afar in the clubs years ago, my entire practical experience in the BDSM world has taken place in the last twelve hours. I'm afraid this is going to be the world's shortest game of truth or dare. If you haven't done it to me, it hasn't been done."

The look on Lukus's face was one of total surprise. When he remained silent she added, "Wow. I've rendered you completely speechless. Amazing."

Still. Silence. She rambled on, trying to fill the awkward silence. "I know, I'm gonna really drag you down. You'll be having to stop and explain so much, and have to treat me with kid gloves while I figure this all out. I totally understand if..."

"Stop. Not one more word." He blurted. For a brief moment, Tiff thought he was really angry with her, until Lukus put on his hot coals smile. "So, you've never been spanked with a belt or a paddle?"

"No." Just thinking about the possibility, though, ratcheted up her heart rate a notch.

"You've never been tied down and played with?"

"Not before last night, no."

"How about blindfolded or gagged?"

"Honey, I told you. If you didn't do it, it hasn't been done. So no to the blindfold but yes to the gag."

He had a true sparkle to his eyes as he continued to probe. "And how'd it make you feel last night when you were tied down and gagged in the audience pit?"

Surely, he didn't need her to answer. Her labored breathing should have been answer enough. Still he waited for her quiet response. "I really liked it... a lot."

"Good girl. So, when I told you you'd earned a punishment for not telling me about Jason, that will truly be your first punishment?"

She was so nervous and excited that she

couldn't get even a simple "yes" out. She finally managed to nod yes to answer his question.

"Oh man. This is going to be so much fun." Lukus suddenly took on the look of a kid in a candy store, which had Tiffany confused.

"You mean you aren't angry? Surely you know you're going to have to go slow for me, right? I'm not sure how I feel about everything yet. I could end up hating it all."

Lukus was chuckling as he answered. "Are you kidding me? You're not gonna hate anything, baby. Not the way I do it. Truly, I never would've said it was important to me until this very minute, but knowing no one else has ever shared the D/s lifestyle with you makes me so happy. I love that this is going to be something special—something that's just ours. I'm honored I get to be the one who'll introduce you to so many new experiences and help you overcome your fear. I'm going take such good care of you and I'll make sure you love every single minute."

Lukus didn't waste any time. He sealed his promise by capturing her mouth with his own. Tiff could feel his cock growing ever harder between their bodies and she was hit with a wave of hot desire. She wanted him buried inside her, filling her completely.

Only then did she realize she'd gotten screwed out of asking Lukus a question for their game, and she'd already thought of exactly what she wanted to ask.

Pressing persistently against his hard chest, Tiff finally got Lukus to pull out of their kiss long enough to peer down into her eyes. She detected a mild annoyance at the interruption.

"We didn't finish the round yet. I get to ask you my question before we can take an intermission." Tiff flashed him a broad smile that won her a return grin. "So Lukus, if you could have me do absolutely anything for you sexually, what's the number one thing you'd like from me, more than anything else?"

"Wow, carte blanche. Anything?"

"Yep. Let me be clear. I'm not promising anything here. I'd just like to know what the Master's Master thinks of as his nirvana."

"Well, coming up with number two would be hard, but number one is easy."

"Yes... and..."

The smile he delivered should've warned her. "I'd love to wake up every morning to you sucking my cock. Some mornings it might be just to get me hot and ready for our first early morning fuck. Other days I'd face-fuck you and force you to swallow every single drop of my cum as I press deep down your throat.

"And on weekends, when we have more time, you could spend an hour worshipping my cock with your tongue, your mouth, your hands, driving me to the edge before I rolled you over and made long, sweet love to you. Basically, I'd love to have you giving me head as my alarm clock every morning. I can't think of a better possible way to start my day."

"Seriously...?"

"You asked."

"You couldn't think of anything better?" she asked incredulously.

"Hey, we have a no lie zone so I told the truth."

"So, is that what you expect?"

"Truthfully?"

"Of course, truthfully, considering the afore mentioned no-lie zone."

"Expect? No. Want? Sure."

"I see."

It was easy to see Lukus had had enough talking. While Tiff was still distracted trying to process his answer, Lukus managed to roll her over onto her tummy, effortlessly lifting her so she was kneeling in the middle of the bed. Lukus took his place directly behind her, pressing his body hard against her naked back. He had full access to her in this position, and he wasted no time in grabbing her right breast in his right hand, squeezing tightly and dragging a moan from his captive. His left hand trekked lower to cup her mound, placing the heel of his hand hard against her clit, as he grinded hard enough to bring her quickly to the edge.

Tiff was just able to reach her arms behind her back, snaking her hands between their bodies to successfully grasp Lukus's growing cock. Hot desire overcame Tiffany as she found her upper body pushed to the bed, leaving her ass high in the air. Lukus used his leg to spread her knees wider apart. She briefly acknowledged to herself she must have made quite a sight for Lukus from behind. He used the tip of his cock to make several swipes up and down her drenched slit, making sure she was ready for him.

Tiffany was holding her breath, knowing his hopefully forceful insertion was only seconds away. When Lukus finally took her, it was in a hard, decisive manner that left no doubt that he was claiming her body as his own. He pulled out slowly, only to crush forward again and again several times, before he unexpectedly stopped, pulling out of Tiff completely.

"Holy fuck. You have me so distracted I forgot to put on a condom. I'm so sorry, baby."

Tiff was hanging by a thread and the abrupt delay of game was unwelcome. She reassured him breathlessly, desperate for him to be back inside her. "It's okay, Lukus. I'm protected. You don't need to use a condom. I won't get pregnant."

She couldn't see his expression from her facedown position, but she felt him moving to the edge of the bed to lean over to the nightstand and grab a foil-wrapped packet. Only then did she realize how much she didn't want him to use a condom. She wanted—no—she *needed* to feel him inside of her. All of him. To feel him shoot his cum deep inside, only to have it drip out in their post-coital snuggling.

"Lukus, please. I promise. You don't need to use a condom, honey."

She heard the reluctance in his voice. "Baby, I can't wait to get rid of them, too. But I haven't been tested in a month and I won't put you at risk. I need to make sure I won't be putting you in danger when I stop using them."

An unwelcome and intense wave of jealously washed over Tiffany at the realization that he needed to be tested because he'd been with so many other partners, he could put her in danger. The truth was a virtual smack across her face, acting as a cold bucket of water. She managed to roll to her side, curling up into a fetal position.

I wonder how many women he's slept with in his life? I can count the number of men I've been with on one hand. Who am I kidding? He's probably with that many women in a week. Hell, down on the stage, he could have that many in one night.

"Alright Tiff. That's enough. No sulking."

"I'm not sulking. I'm just tired. I think we should go back to sleep."

In the blink of an eye, Lukus had her flat on her back, trapping her as he straddled her at the waist. He quickly wrestled her arms high and wide, pinning her to the bed as he hovered over her. Tiffany felt his hard tool pressing between their bodies, but it was the hard glint in his eyes that kept her attention. She could feel his dominating gaze seeping through every inch of her body, leaving a warm glow in its wake.

"You're a terrible liar, baby and so you'd better be warned. I know I promised to go slow, but this exquisite ass of yours is about to find out how serious I am about punishing you for lying. So, tell me—now—what's going through that beautiful head of yours?"

Tiff knew she should be happy for a last reprieve, but there was a small part of her that was aware of why she was so on edge. She knew it was only a matter of time before Lukus took things to the next level, and there was a part of her that wondered if it might just be easier to get it over with, to feel the sting of his hand on her ass and find out once and for all how the intense feelings of desire she felt when reading about or watching another woman's submissive punishment translated to her real world. Before meeting Lukus, it had been a casual curiosity. Now she knew her reaction to—and tolerance for—punishments would make or break their budding relationship.

Unwilling to risk finding an answer she might have regretted, she submitted truthfully. "You know why I'm upset, Lukus. I know I have no right whatsoever to feel this way, but I find myself wanting to scratch the eyes out of every woman you've been with before tonight. I'm not naive and it's completely unreasonable, but it's how I feel." Now that he had her talking, she was on a roll. Her voice was escalating. "Worse yet, I know it's not even possible to track them all down because I somehow suspect the number is at minimum in double-digits—hell, it may be triple-digits over your lifetime—and that alone totally freaks me out."

His smug grin was irritating. "Thank you."

"For what? Being an irrational green-eyed twit?"

His hearty laugh had a calming effect. "No, Tiffany. For telling the truth, even though you didn't want to. For what it's worth, I want you to know that no one's ever made me feel like you do. Tonight, is special. Now come here. I'm gonna reward you."

"So, you're taking the condom off? I really do want to feel your cum inside me, Lukus."

Tiff could see his eyes this time as he hovered over her, still restraining her limbs. She saw the flash of temptation before the resolve returned. "Don't push me. I'll always do what I need to do to keep you safe."

Talk time was over. Lukus dove down to suck her nipple into his mouth while still pinning her immobile against the bed. All thoughts of jealousy evaporated as he worked his magic on her body. He had her primed and ready for him again in no time. Rather than simply taking her as they were lying, Lukus maneuvered her back to her hands and knees before pulling her upper body to himself, leaving them pressed flush against each other as they knelt in the middle of his massive bed.

Lukus had the advantage as her back pressed against his muscular chest, leaving his hands free to roam between her full breasts and exposed pussy and every inch of her skin in between. In her hazed excitement, Tiff threw her head back against his shoulder, turning to suck and kiss his neck as he rolled her nipples between his fingers, pinching slightly harder and harder. Tiff kept waiting for the pain to become unbearable, but it never happened. There was only pleasure.

She wondered if she was imagining things when she felt Lukus trembling, but she had no time to evaluate it before he pushed her back to all fours and plunged his cock into her hard, filling her completely in one fluid insertion. Lukus's loud grunts as he fucked her hard mixed with her sexually charged whimpers as he set a punishingly fast pace.

Tiff was vaguely aware of the nearly obscene sounds filling the room as their bodies slapped hard against each other. She felt him lean forward, capturing her wrists in his hands and forcefully pulling her hands out from under her, mashing her face into the bed while he pulled her arms back to trap them in one hand at the small of her back. The submissive position, along with his forceful fucking, combined to drive her to the edge of the cliff, ready to free-fall into a powerful orgasm with just a few more thrusts. She was so close, but it was an unexpected forceful spank to her bare ass with Lukus's strong right hand that threw her over the edge.

She felt his second solid slap connecting with her exposed bottom just as her pussy began to convulse with powerful contractions, gripping Lukus's thick cock harder as his hand rained down yet again in the same tender place on her butt.

"Fuck yeah, Tiff. That's it, baby. Squeeze me. Come for me again."

Tiffany's whimpers turned into a full-fledged scream as Lukus's hand connected with her ass with the hardest swat yet. In her orgasmic haze, she felt Lukus still himself while seated deep inside of her. She realized he'd stopped, thinking he was hurting her.

"Oh, no... don't stop! I need more. Please, Lukus... again."

She heard what sounded like a relieved whoosh as he pulled completely out of her body before thrusting forward hard and fast. He fucked her thoroughly, bringing her ever closer to her next release before switching hands to spank her left ass cheek in the same way he had her right just minutes before. This time she couldn't contain her rant as she drove over the cliff, free-falling again.

"Oh yes, honey. Thank you! That's it! I want more... more... more!"

Tiffany's guttural pleas were coming in rhythm with Lukus's thrusts. He managed to add playful swats to her reddening ass in the same perfect rhythm until he'd driven over the cliff himself. Grabbing both of her hips tightly, he buried himself as deep inside her as he could, shooting hot ropes of cum into the resented condom.

Lukus stayed deep inside her as he caught his breath before finally managing to flop them over onto their sides and spooning Tiff tightly against him. Tiff could hear how labored his breath was, and knew he got a good workout servicing her so intimately. They remained silently locked together long enough for his now flaccid cock to slip out of Tiffany's wet folds. It was just moments before she detected the slow even breathing of a sleeping Lukus.

Tiff quietly extricated herself from his protective arms long enough to remove the offending condom, tossing it into the nearby wastebasket on her way to the bathroom. She turned on a small spotlight over the whirlpool tub to avoid glaring brightness as she readied a warm washcloth she planned to use first on her face and then to clean up Lukus's cum-covered cock when she returns to bed.

I have plans for him in the morning.

Catching a glimpse of herself in the mirror, she was stunned to see the sex-mussed, confidently sated woman staring back. It was hard to believe it'd only been a few short hours since she was last standing here willing herself to stay calm in light of finding Lukus's treasure chest of sex toys. She'd gotten answers to so many questions in the last few hours. She said a quiet prayer of thanks that she'd been brave enough to stay—brave enough to retire as a voyeur and plunge into real life.

As if needing proof that the last few amazing hours hadn't just been some figment of her imagination, Tiff turned her body so she could see her ass in the reflection of the long mirror. The faint hand marks marking her were real. It was the proof she needed to know she was now on a new path.

I guess I got my answer. If a real spanking is anything close to how wonderful those swats were, he can spank me every single day. The man is truly amazing.

CHAPTER SIX

BRIANNA

Brianna stirred awake as the rays of early morning sunlight peeked through the wall of bedroom windows. Between the sun and her naked husband pressed tightly against her back, Bri was toasty warm and utterly content. The only thing that could make this morning better would be if Markus were still seated inside of her.

Bri took the quiet time to reflect back on the last few event-filled days. While things may have turned out okay in the end, she knew just how lucky she was Markus had forgiven her for her foolish and dangerous actions. In fact, it was better than simply being forgiven. The truth about her secret sexual desires was finally out in the open and instead of being angry, Markus was prepared to take his place as not only her husband, but now her Dom and Head of the House (HoH) as well.

But, beneath her calm facade, her guilt was still

there, reminding her she may not deserve to be forgiven after her truly unforgivable act of infidelity. The fact Markus was able to put the whole incident behind them made her that much more grateful to have him in her life.

And she owed all her thanks to one man—one sexy, extraordinary man—Lukus Mitchell. While the well-deserved punishments she'd suffered at his hands had been frightening and painful, she knew it was the depth of his experience in the BDSM lifestyle that had made him the perfect person to help save her marriage. If Lukus hadn't recognized her own need to be dominated and gone out of his way to enlighten Markus about the secret needs of his wayward wife, Bri knew this weekend would be ending very differently. Without Lukus's help, she most likely would have been moving out of the home she shared with Markus in the suburbs as he began divorce proceedings. Instead, she was lying in her husband's arms, the feel of his corrective punishment still warming her bottom, reminding her she was very lucky and loved.

The fact she'd been married to Markus for over three years and never met his best friend spoke volumes to Brianna about just how desperately Markus had wanted to conceal his past life as a Dom to his first wife, Georgie from her. Reflecting back to their discussion the night before, Bri had to admit it was both exciting and troubling at the same time to know Markus was capable of such strong domination. Last night she got just a glimpse of him in a role she'd only dreamed of, and it was both thrilling and scary to think about how their marriage was going to change as they started down this new path together. They'd always enjoyed a good sex life, but Bri could only imagine how much better it was going to get with the addition of dominance and submission.

"Good morning, beautiful. Penny for your thoughts."

Bri had been so lost, she'd missed her husband rousing awake. She felt him hugging her tighter against his body and giggled when she felt his semi-hard erection already growing against her ass.

"Good morning, Markus. I was just thinking about how lucky I am."

"I'm guessing your poor ass isn't feeling quite as lucky this morning and if it is, maybe I didn't do a good enough job punishing you last night."

"Oh, no. You definitely did a good enough job. Between you and Lukus, I'm pretty sure my ass isn't going to get back to normal for a few days."

"Sorry, but I think you're gonna have to get used to a new normal, my dear." Markus nibbled on her neck as he snuggled in closer.

Bri chuckled softly. "I was just thinking about that too, Sir."

"Damn, I love hearing you say that, sweetheart." Markus allowed his right hand to find the swell of her hip, gently stroking down to her ass, his touch possessive.

"I love saying it. It still feels a bit like a dream. Like I'm going to wake up and be back down in that cage."

"I wish you'd stop reminding me of that. God, I was a complete ass to leave you here alone, knowing what you were gonna go through."

"Markus, let's not go over this again. I understand how upset you were. I deserved what happened to me. It's what had to happen for us to not only get past my infidelity, but more importantly it set things in motion for us to understand how we need to introduce D/s into our marriage. How else could you have ever forgiven me?"

With a sigh, Markus sat up, flipping her onto her back, quickly lifting her arms above her head, sitting across her waist, trapping her against the bed in a flash. "You're right of course, but I still don't have to like it. In fact, speaking of forgiving, we agreed there would be no more secrets. I meant it when I said last night that all was forgiven. And it is. But there's one more thing that's still bothering me that we haven't talked about yet. I need to get it off my chest because it really hurt me."

Bri could see the flicker of anger cross his face and knew she'd been too optimistic thinking they could put her infidelity behind them so quickly. He may have forgiven her, but *forgetting...* that would take a lot longer.

I'm going to do whatever it takes to make it up to him.

Markus let several tense seconds pass by before finally voicing his concern. "How many times have I asked you to try anal sex?"

Bri's heart rate shot up. She should have anticipated this. "I don't know, honey, but I know what you're thinking."

"Do you? I somehow doubt it."

"I didn't ask him to—really. I've always said, 'no.' He didn't listen."

"I don't give a shit. That was mine, Brianna. That bastard took what's mine."

Brianna's heart raced, unfortunately remembering the agony Jake had inflicted on her body. Seeing the anger in her husband's eyes made that pain worse. If he knew the whole truth, would it even make a difference?

She hesitated, afraid to open a whole new can of worms, but then chastised herself for even considering keeping more secrets from the man she loved. Bri took a deep breath and dived into her reply. "I hate it, but I think we should talk about what you heard when you were listening in with Lukus." She paused as his eyes widened, clearly not expecting her to bring it up.

"Why would you want to talk about that?" Markus asked, anger blazing in his eyes.

Brianna refrained from reminding him that he had been the one to bring the subject up. Instead, she reached up to softly cup his stubbled face just inches away. "Honey, I thought we weren't going to avoid talking about the hard stuff." Her words dowsed his anger, leaving only appreciation in his eyes.

"Damn, you're right. I hate it, but we can't pretend I didn't hear what I heard. That a part of me died listening you coming while he..."

That hearing his wife having sex with another man hurt him did not surprise Brianna. But, the unknown at the moment, was if telling him exactly what *had* happened in that room would make her husband feel better, or worse.

"I know this is gonna sound crazy, but I wish you and Lukus had started listening earlier... or even could have been watching too, not just listening. Maybe then you'd have been able to see..." Bri's voice trailed off, suddenly unsure how Markus would take the news.

"Trust me, Bri. Hearing you coming was bad enough."

"So, Lukus didn't tell you, did he?" she asked, quietly. She'd love to blame Lukus, but this was her mess to clean up. He'd done enough. The angry confusion on his face was her answer so she forged ahead. "What was the first thing you heard?"

"I heard enough," Markus insisted, agitated.

"What was the first thing?" she questioned, more pointed this time.

"The belting. You moaning again and again. Him calling me Vanilla and saying only he knew how to make you come. Him talking about lubing up your ass. I know what you sound like when you come. Don't tell me you didn't orgasm, Bri." He was close to shouting by the time he'd finished his long list of dastardly deeds.

Bri stroked his face softly, waiting for him to calm again before saying words she suspected would hurt him, that was if he even believed her. "So you didn't hear me demanding the hard drive?" When he didn't answer, she continued. "Or me crying out, hoping to get the attention of someone passing by in the hall of the hotel? Or him tackling me and laughing as he tied me up and put duct tape over my mouth to keep me quiet?"

Markus closed his eyes, just inches above her. He shook his head as he forced himself to recall. The pain in his voice as he relived what he'd heard was real. "I don't remember hearing your voice at all until... He kept calling you his slut... saying how tight... how perfect you were together. I heard you coming. Then it got really quiet and I thought you'd left, but I tried calling you and could hear the ringing so I knew you were still there. Then later, I could hear muffled talking, but it must have been farther away from your purse because I couldn't hear what was said. Then the door slammed and all I could hear was you crying."

Only after he finished his memories did he open his painfilled eyes. They sat in silence for a few long seconds before he asked, "What does Lukus know that I don't?"

"It doesn't really matter. I was stupid enough to go there..."

"Brianna. What am I missing?"

"I didn't go there to cheat on you, Markus. I went there because he's blackmailing me."

"Blackmail? Why the fuck wouldn't you come to me with that?" He yelled directly into her face.

She rushed to explain. "Because, he has pictures. Videos. Terrible shit from the past that would hurt you—hurt *us*. I was stupid. I should have known it was just a trap. But once he got me behind closed doors... there was nothing I could do. He's just too strong."

"Too strong? Wait. What are you saying? You didn't want him to tie you up and belt you?"

Brianna had to be truthful, as much as it hurt. "I'd love to blame all this on Jake because I was absolutely not a willing participant this time, but the fact is I did go with him once a long time ago. He has photos. It's how he lured me there this time."

"So, if you didn't... but you came. I heard you."

"I did, and I hate myself for it, but..."

Darkness turned her husband's beautiful brown

eyes almost black as he silently thought through what she'd said. For the briefest of moments, she worried his newfound anger was directed at her and she panicked, worried she'd already ruined their precarious reunion.

"Rape?" Markus said the hated word she'd refused to use herself. She couldn't formulate a response as the ugly word hung between them until Markus's tortured revelation. "You mean I just sat there, listening to you being raped?" His voice cracked as perspiration gathered on his brow.

The pain in his eyes took her back to the night he'd left her in the box at the Punishment Pit. It was an agony she'd prayed she'd never see again on her handsome husband's face. Like that night, she rushed to try to ease his pain.

"Honey, please. I was stupid to go there with him. I know what he's capable of."

"Are you actually defending him?" Markus pushed up, flailing above her as his anger grew.

Bri reached out wrap her arms around her husband's neck, trying her best to hold him close. "Of course not! I hate him with every fiber of my being. But that doesn't change the fact that with the exception of the anal sex, what he did to me in that hotel room wasn't any different than what he's done to me dozens of times over the years."

"Fuck, I thought I hated him yesterday. How the hell are you acting so calmly?" He gritted the words out as if they brought him pain.

"I guess because what he did to me wasn't even close to as bad as the pain I felt knowing I'd hurt you. Knowing I'd risked our marriage. As long as you and I come through this okay, what Jake did to me is old news."

"Maybe for you, but not for me. Not by a long shot."

Brianna scrambled to think of a way to bring their hard conversation back around to their reunion. To their renewed commitment to their marriage and each other.

"I know one way you can make both of us feel better," she offered.

"I sincerely doubt that, unless you tell me Davenport is behind bars... or better yet, six feet under."

God, I pray he doesn't mean that. As much as I want Jake to pay, I don't want Markus to do something reckless that will get him in trouble with the law.

She did her best to bring their earlier playfulness back. "I was thinking more along the lines of you... well... you know..."

"Bri, I don't know shit anymore."

"That's too bad. I was hoping you could show me how anal sex is really supposed to be with someone you love."

That got his attention. His brown eyes locked on her gaze from above. "You can't be serious. Now.

In the middle of this heavy discussion, you want to distract me? With sex?"

"Actually, with *anal* sex. And yes." She flashed her husband her brightest smile.

He didn't dare laugh, or even smile, but she noticed a new lightness back in his eyes as he cautioned her. "I was actually contemplating spanking you all over again for keeping all this important information from me last night."

Her heart rate took off at a trot at the thought of her sexy husband disciplining her. She'd only dreamed of it before. That it was a reality seemed impossible.

Working to distract him from the darkness they'd been discussing, she teased, "Maybe you should do both? A spanking for punishment and then you could take my ass to show me who it really belongs to."

He finally couldn't hide a small smile as he lectured her. "Mrs. Lambert, I do believe this is the textbook definition of topping from the bottom."

Bri sat up just far enough to give him a quick and playful kiss before asking, "Is it working?"

His laughter was like medicine. His kiss, her favorite remedy for anything wrong in her life. And his erection coming to life pressing against her stomach as they made out—that was going to be her reward.

Before she knew what was happening, Markus

broke their kiss and rolled to the edge of the bed, pulling her along with him. She wasn't really sure what he was up to until he pulled her to the corner of the room to a large comfortable-looking cushioned chair with an oversized ottoman. Under different circumstances, it looked like the kind of a chair Bri could lose herself in for a few hours, reading a good romance novel. Today, she suspected that wasn't what Markus had in mind. He released her hand long enough to push the chair out into the middle of the bedroom before reaching back to grasp her hand again, pulling her forward.

"I thought about taking you down to the stage this morning to use some of Lukus's punishment furniture, but I'd rather not wait. We can improvise."

Only now did it really dawn on her what she'd been suggesting, and she panicked. After all she only had the painful episode with Jake as a frame of reference. "Maybe we should wait to do this when we get home, later."

Markus framed her face in his hands, holding it, and her gaze, firmly in place. "I realize it's gonna take us both some time to get used to the changes in the dynamics of our marriage, Brianna, but you seem to forget I'm your Dom now. Or was this all just a game to you?"

His question caught her off guard and Bri was suddenly lightheaded. "It's no game, Markus." She could hear the tremble in her voice as she softly answered.

"S*ir*. When we're in the bedroom or talking about either sex or punishments, I'm S*ir*... unless..."

The pause was long enough that she had to ask. "Unless what?"

"Unless you're looking for a Master. We haven't really talked about the nuances between M/s and D/s yet, and honestly, I'm too impatient this morning. That discussion can wait, but we *are* going to have it... and soon."

Bri was relieved. They had already covered too many heavy topics this morning. She confirmed with a simple, "Yes, Sir."

"Good girl. Now, do you trust me?"

That was an easy question. "Of course, I trust you."

"Do you really? Because when you argue back, it seems to me like you don't trust me to know what's best for you. Whose decision is it to decide what we're going to do this morning?"

Brianna's breathing was getting labored. She'd waited for years for her husband to take charge of her, to dominate her and take what belonged to him, to protect her and hold her accountable, to punish her when she needed correction. As frightening as the idea was, she couldn't deny the warm glow she felt as Markus asserted his authority.

"It's your decision, Sir."

"That's right, it is. I've decided I've waited long enough to claim my wife's ass. I need to replace any memory you have of what that fucker did to your body."

Letting go of her face, Markus pulled Bri forward, quickly draping her body across the low-backed cushioned chair. It was the perfect height for her to lie across as it lifted her ass up high while still allowing her feet to stay on the ground. Her face was mashed into the seat cushions and she immediately felt open and vulnerable.

Bri was hit by a sudden panic. "Sir, please. At least let me go freshen up for you... I mean... what if..."

"I couldn't care less, Brianna."

"But, I haven't showered since yesterday afternoon. I really think..."

With a series of quick slaps to her punished ass, Markus cut her off. "I said *enough*. I'm going to take you exactly as you are."

She heard Markus walking away and used the time alone to conjure up the submissive feelings she'd felt the night before—her desire to be dominated ran so deep she'd risked everything.

I need this. He isn't going to hurt me. He loves me. He may push my limits, but Markus is never going to hurt me.

He was back too quickly. She was surprised when he grabbed her wrists and pulled her arms behind her back, leaving little support for her body, causing the urge to pee. Most of her weight was now pressing down on her bladder, which happened to be exactly where the chair was supporting her. She was going to have to fight to hold it because she knew better than to ask again to go to the bathroom.

She felt Markus attaching leather cuffs to each wrist and then linking them together, securing her arms immobile behind her back. She couldn't see anything from her vantage point and only had her senses of hearing and touch to go by. He grasped her left ankle to cuff it to the base of the chair—making her open and immobile. As Markus attached her right ankle, desire coursed through Bri's body as she mentally prepared to be claimed by her husband in the most primal way.

It was comforting when Markus began to massage her ass gently, taking time to admire some of the remaining welts from her previous punishments. Bri was hit with a confusing feeling of pride that she'd been able to take her punishment like a good girl.

His hand left her ass just long enough to gather up some lube, and the next sensation Bri felt was that of his finger pressing at the entrance of her most private hole. She could feel him sliding the slick lube around her anus before gently inserting one finger up to his first knuckle. A moan escaped her at the invasion, and she had to admit, so far it felt fantastic.

Markus spent several long minutes intimately preparing his wife to take his cock. He used plenty of lube and continuously pushed her limits by going deeper and adding additional fingers until he was finally giving her ass a fast finger fuck.

"That's my naughty little girl. You like it, don't you?"

Her breath was labored. "Oh God yes, Sir. I'm your naughty girl."

"Am I hurting you? If it starts to hurt, you need to say 'yellow' and I'll slow down."

"It doesn't hurt. It just feels so... I don't know how to describe it. It feels... weird, I guess."

Markus was chuckling. "Weird, you say? I was hoping for something closer to *good*, maybe even *wonderful*."

"How about *full*?"

"Oh, sweetheart. You're not even close to full yet, but you will be in a minute. Oh yeah, I think you're just about ready for me."

His naughty promise had her pussy creaming. While the ass fingering felt good, her poor clit was feeling neglected and she doubted very much that she was going to be one of those rare women she'd read about who could actually orgasm from anal sex only. Still, she was excited to give Markus this final part of her body. After all they'd been through in the last few days, it felt right to be giving this most private part of herself to him while submissively restrained. It was the perfect demonstration of how drastically their relationship was changing. The old Markus never would've asserted himself after her first objection.

She could feel Markus lining up behind her. The lube lathered his rock-hard cock as he pressed the head against her puckered opening. He began inserting gently before cautioning her.

"Relax, Bri. Let me in. I'm gonna take it slow, but I *am* going to come deep in your ass this morning."

She focused on relaxing and felt him pushing forward to slowly fill her, millimeter by millimeter. Once the head of his cock was past her tight ring, the invasion got easier. The physical feelings of fullness were amazing enough, but the emotional tidal wave would have knocked Bri on her ass were it not for the chair's support. There was something so humbling about having her ass fucked as Markus slid deeper. The sensation was borderline painful yet, somehow, she was able to accommodate him.

With relief, she finally felt his balls pressing against her pussy and she knew he was finally all the way in. He held still, allowing her ass to become accustomed to the invasion. While he held, balls deep, he grabbed her hips possessively before easing out an inch or two before slowly edging forward again and again.

"You're so fucking tight, Brianna. You feel like a vise grip on my cock. I can't even tell you how much this is turning me on. Not just how good you feel; you should see how beautiful you look right now. Your ass is still red and welted from your punishment. I can see you opening up to take all of me deep. The only thing better would be if I could see your eyes right now. There'll be mirrors the next time so I can watch every emotion on your face as you take me deep. Are you ready?"

"Yes, Sir. I'm ready." Her breath was quick and shallow.

"What are you ready for? Ask me for it."

"Please..."

"Please, what?

He'd pushed her to the edge and she was finding coherent thoughts hard to form. Forming words was even harder. "Please... just fuck me. Fuck my ass, Markus."

Through the silence, the next sound she detected was the swish of moving air just before Markus's hand connected with her tender right ass cheek. The hard swat was unexpected and immediately ignited feelings of both pain and pleasure.

"Oweeeee!"

"Want to try that again?"

Bri realized her error. "I'm sorry, Sir. Please, fuck my ass, Sir. No... please fuck *your* ass, Sir."

"Perfect. That's my good girl. Hold tight, sweetheart."

She felt him pulling away from her body and the brief emptiness was disarming. In no time, she felt him pressing forward, faster than before, pushing inside in one strong insertion. The power of it took her breath away. She had no time to react as he pulled out and thrusted forward again, until he was fucking her in earnest, pulling her hips hard to make sure he hit deep inside her.

In all her life, Brianna had never felt like she felt that moment. It wasn't that it hurt or even felt bad—it was just that getting fucked in her most private orifice just felt so naughty, so *dirty*. To have her husband buried deep in her ass was the ultimate in submission for Brianna. The fullness, combined with the pressure on her bladder and being immobilized, had Brianna dripping wet. She could actually feel her pussy throbbing, desperate for some attention.

The manly grunting sounds Markus was making as he claimed what was his only added to her own excitement. She could feel his long strokes getting harder and faster and knew he was getting close to coming. She wanted so bad to touch her own clit, and eventually had to ask for her release.

"Can you please play with my clit, Sir? I want so bad to come with you, but I'm not going to be able to come without you touching me."

He was winded from his exertion. "Oh, sweetheart. I want you to come, but I have a better idea."

She had no time to understand his intention until she felt the slap of his hand on her ass cheek.

He began her spanking, holding nothing back. Given that her ass was already tender, each connection packed a powerful punch, and for the pain slut that she was the punches had a direct line to her core. She was flying higher and higher with each hard slap to her bottom and in no time, she was on the brink of an orgasm.

"Are you ready to come with me, sweetheart? I'm gonna come in this tight ass of yours."

"Oh God.... yes... fuck me hard... I need it so bad!"

"Come, baby." And with his final command, Bri felt him leaning against her back, sliding his left hand over her mound and putting hard pressure on her clit, rubbing it masterfully. The sensations merged to throw her into a strong climax just as she felt the contractions of his cock depositing cum deep in her bowels. She vaguely heard her own passionate cry as she let the wave of ecstasy wash over her.

Oh my freaking God, that was awesome! We should have been doing that years ago!

Apparently, Markus was as affected by his powerful orgasm as Bri, because he lay heavy across her back, letting the chair support them both.

Brianna had to squeeze out her request. "Markus, please. I really have to pee. Can you lean up?"

Reluctantly, her husband pushed himself off her, but stayed close enough to remain buried in her depths. The tender, soft strokes across her lower back were comforting and intimate, reminding Brianna this man connected to her intimately was more than her Dom—he was the man of her dreams.

Eventually, Markus gently withdrew from his wife's body. She couldn't see him, but she could feel he remained close. It was silly considering they'd been married for three years, but she was suddenly shy and embarrassed because she knew he was standing there, admiring her thoroughly fucked, gaping hole. He confirmed her suspicion when he said, "Absolutely beautiful," before unlocking first her wrist and then ankle cuffs.

Markus helped her slowly right herself and then swept her into his arms and headed to the bathroom. Brianna snuggled into the crook of his neck as she threw her arms around him. She'd never felt more loved in her entire life than she did at this very minute. After coming so very close to losing her marriage, she knew she'd never again take it for granted. The man cradling her in his muscular arms was it for her.

As he slowly lowered her legs to the floor next to the shower, she tightened her grip around his neck. Holding him close, she spilled out her heart.

"I love you so much, Markus."

"I know, Bri. I love you too, but you do know things are going to be different. No more secrets."

"Yes, I know. No more secrets."

"Okay. Time for a shower. I'm starving and I can't wait to get you home so we can spend the afternoon in bed."

Brianna's heart skipped. "That sounds like heaven."

CHAPTER SEVEN

LUKUS

Lukus was having the best dream he'd had in a long time. It was so incredible, he didn't want to pry his sleep-heavy eyes open, in spite of the bright sunlight he felt hitting his face.

Just a few more minutes before I have to wake up and let it end.

The feel of the slave girl licking his dick like a cherished lollypop was heavenly, and considering how long it'd been since he'd had a top-notch blowjob, he wanted to let the dream last as long as possible. In his sleepy haze, Lukus missed the first telltale signs that this was something much more than a dream.

Only when he heard a familiar moan did he jolt awake, immediately snapping his eyes open while propping the top half of his body up on his elbows. His now fully awake consciousness took in the splendid vision of a naked Tiffany, kneeling submissively between his legs. She had the base of his hard cock firmly in her left hand, stroking him, while she used her tongue like a pro, teasing the pre-cum from his slit with a gentle swish of her tongue before opening wide to suck the first few inches of his shaft into her warm mouth.

Holy fuck, she's giving me my alarm-clock wish.

Lukus closed his eyes while emitting a blissful groan, throwing his head back and taking a long minute to simply enjoy the feel of Tiffany's intimate morning wake-up call. His heart rate synched with the thrusts of his dick into her wet mouth.

After enjoying a few minutes of tactile heaven, Lukus's physical desire took a back seat to his visual desire. As he re-opened his eyes, he took another long minute to simply admire her. With her facing him, he had an unfettered view as Tiffany's heavy breasts swung in time with her sucking strokes. Lukus wished his arms were long enough to reach out and squeeze her perky tits, but he was too content to sit up.

"Eyes. I want to see your eyes, baby."

If he hadn't already been lying down, the expression shining back at him as she slowly raised her eyes to meet his gaze would have had the power to knock him on his ass. Her eyes were shining with a perfect mix of innocence, submission, and sass. Truly, he'd never known any other woman who could convey so much with eye contact alone, and right now her peepers told him she was very much enjoying giving him a little slice of his nirvana. In fact, she paused her thrusts just long enough to let her mouth, completely full of hard flesh, form into the most mischievous, if somewhat lopsided, smile.

Oh, you little minx. You know exactly what you're doing, don't you?

A pang of something close to jealously hit Lukus as he had an unwelcome vision of her practicing in the past by waking up Justin, or Jeffrey, or whatever the fuck his name was with this same personal treatment. The emotions the stray thought stirred were foreign to the Dom. Hell, he'd always been more than willing to share the women he'd been with, often times allowing other Doms to partake of his sub-of-the-week on stage while he watched.

It was not lost on him that he'd previously taken pride in his utter lack of jealousy where women were concerned, going so far as to privately ridicule Masters who would guard their subs so closely, they'd never allow anyone to so much as touch them. The fact he was pretty sure he'd gut the first guy to touch a hair on Tiff's head told him just how much trouble he might be getting himself into.

These new feelings had Lukus off-base and in a very uncharacteristic unguarded moment, he let his first thought blurt out, his jealous resentment seeping into his tone. "You're pretty good at this,

Tiff. I'd love to know more about all the men you've been practicing on? Seems like you've really been able to hone your oral skills."

He saw a quick flicker of hurt flash through her eyes, but it was immediately pushed aside by unmistakable anger. She quickly knelt up, letting his now free, hard cock slap back against his muscular stomach with a wet plop. He could see he'd made a tactical mistake with his careless comment.

"Seriously? This coming from the man who had to use a condom last night because he's been with so many other women, he might put me at risk. Can you say 'hypocrite'?" There were almost visible sparks flying off Tiff as she let him have it.

Lukus was stunned into a brief silence. He was not exactly sure who he was most angry with at the moment—himself for being such an insensitive clod, or Tiffany for daring to talk to him in that sassy tone. He had to take a deep breath to collect his thoughts before he made things even worse.

When he spoke, he was back in control. "Be careful, little girl. You may be right—I was an ass to say that, but that doesn't give you the right to talk to me in that tone."

"The hell it doesn't, Lukus. I realize you may be used to women cowering at your feet, ready to blindly do your bidding without talking back, but I'm afraid you're going to have to actually earn the right to expect that from me. You were right last night and I *loved* that you didn't let me get away with sulking and acting like a jealous bitch. Well buddy, the shoe's on the other foot. I'm not gonna let you get away with purposefully hurting or humiliating me. If you say something stupid, I'm going call you on it—in *or* out of the bedroom. I think you need to decide if you're going to be able to live with that."

To help make her point, Tiff crossed her arms in front of her chest as she glared down on Lukus lying before her. She was clearly waiting to see if he was going to acquiesce. As they had their showdown, he detected an increasing trembling in her limbs, yet she somehow managed to maintain her composure while staring down at him.

Damn, she's good at this.

He should have been furious with her for talking to him like she did, for standing up to him and in his bedroom—hell, in his *bed*, no less. As Lukus truthfully examined his emotions, he found fury was not among the dangerous mix of feelings coursing through him. Anger, yes, but not all of it was aimed at the beautiful blonde with the sex-messed hair and swollen lips who was not-so-patiently waiting for a reply.

More than anger, he had to acknowledge the strongest sentiment coursing through him was excitement that he'd found a woman with an amazing mix of strength and submission, of tenacity and vulnerability, of lusty sexiness and tender innocence. How she managed to wrap all of the divergent parts of herself together in that amazingly beautiful wrapper was a mystery to Lukus, but he knew one thing for damn sure—he'd be the biggest idiot ever to let her get away from him. With that simple realization, a strange calm settled into the Dom's chest and he knew what he needed to do.

"Tiffany. You're right. I'm sorry."

She could barely contain her surprise at his words. Her deflating sigh exposed just how afraid she'd been that her gamble would cost her a budding relationship. Now that she'd won, she looked unsure how to proceed.

It was clear to Lukus she hadn't expected him to apologize, and it made him even more glad he had. He took advantage of her momentary confusion to take back control. Quickly sitting up and hugging her to him, he managed to roll them over to the far side of the king-sized bed, trapping Tiffany beneath him, their faces just a few inches apart.

"Now, Miss O'Sullivan, I'd like to get back to where we were before I carelessly ruined the mood. I love that you woke me up like that and I'm sorry I had a moment of—what did you call it last night—being a green-eyed twit? Can we agree I'm more like a green-eyed lion? My roar can be a bit much at times, I know. And anyway, 'twit' just doesn't seem to fit me at all." He let a mischievous smile play at his lips as he sought to win her over, and knew she'd forgiven him when she taunted him back.

"I think I'll stick with a shark—a rather large-toothed, green-eyed, circling shark. I still feel like I'm swimming in the deep end of the tank with every conversation we have, Lukus."

Lukus let his smile turn predatory. "Well, you're proving to be an excellent swimmer, baby. Never fear. You're safe from the shark, at least for now."

Lukus swooped in to capture her mouth in a tender kiss and then was surprised when she tried to pull away.

"Hold on. I need to go brush my teeth. I have morning breath."

"Who the hell cares? So do I. Anyway, it's time to restart where you left off with my morning wake-up call."

Lukus rolled off Tiff to lie on his back, giving her access to his semi-hard erection again. When she didn't move to resume his blowjob, he turned in time to see her with a naughty smile adorning her face.

"I see. You're gonna play hard to get now, is that it?"

"Well things didn't work out so hot when I took charge."

"I can solve that problem."

Lukus rolled, quickly lifting Tiffany's arms

above her head. "Hold onto the headboard rails, baby. Don't let go."

He added another pillow under her head, lifting her face to a forty-five degree angle from the bed. Moving to the head of the bed, he swung his leg over Tiffany's body in a way that put his cock right in front of her mouth. He looked down, his eyes locking with Tiffany's own lust-filled gaze as he held onto the headboard himself to keep from putting too much weight on her. He liked that this position put him in complete control over not only the tempo, but also the depth of his thrusts into Tiffany's waiting mouth.

Placing the tip of his cock against her lips, Lukus coaxed her. "Open up, baby."

She opened her mouth slightly, sticking her tongue out to tentatively lick his dick. He allowed her time to become accustomed to the position before pushing forward, forcing several inches of expanding flesh into her warm mouth. She hadn't taken her eyes off his and once again, he could see the emotions racing across her face.

Several minutes went by with Lukus slowly... gently... playing with Tiff, allowing her plenty of time to lick and suck while he enjoyed the slow build up. The growing intimacy between them was working its magic to connect them in ways much more profound than skin deep. There was something special about staring into the eyes of this amazing woman as she had his cock in her mouth.

It shook a deep, dormant place awake inside Lukus. He'd had dozens of women perform this very same act on him over the years, but not once had it felt like this. In the past, it'd always been about two things—dominance and sexual release. Today, there was an important third ingredient added to the mix; it was the unfamiliar emotional connection to Tiff that was making it extraordinary.

Her eyes broadcasted when she was ready for more. He began to push farther with each thrust, holding himself deeper inside her mouth and waiting longer after each pass before pulling out. Lukus watched her reactions carefully. He was trying to gauge her comfort level, looking for the moment where she'd panic because she couldn't breathe freely or when she began to gag on his tool. Lukus's job as a Dom was to push her just *past* that line.

When Tiff closed her eyes, he quickly corrected her. "Open. Always open, baby."

Tiff immediately complied. Her pupils flared at his command. Her submissive expression gave an addictive rush to the Dom. He needed more. "That's it. You need to trust me now. I'm gonna push you, but know I'll never hurt you."

She couldn't talk with her mouth full, but he saw her trust in him shining in her eyes as he pressed deeper, holding longer. The gagging sounds as she struggled to take him deeper and deeper was like an aphrodisiac for Lukus. He pulled out, allowing her to take a deep, gasping breath and was further excited by the string of drool he saw keeping his cock connected to her mouth. A sudden surge of power overcame him as he thrust forward again, pressing deeper into her tight throat.

"Good girl. Swallow me, deeper." Her eyes were watering, serving to only enhance her vulnerability before him. He watched the stray tear trek down her cheek as he reached down with his left hand to gently stroke her sex-mussed hair, his intimacy in direct contrast to the deep-throat fucking he was giving her. After letting her take another gasping breath, Lukus held the back of Tiff's head with his next strong insertion, holding her face immobile—unable to pull away from the thick intrusion invading her throat. Panic flared in her eyes as he pressed deeper.

"It's okay. Breathe through your nose. I've got you."

He heard her following his direction and could see the panic receding from her eyes as she received the precious air. The panic was replaced with a pleased satisfaction that she was able to follow his direction. She swallowed and the squeezing of his cock in her tight throat almost pushed him over the edge. He hated he was already getting close to shooting his wad. He wanted to make this last for hours. The gurgling noises Tiff was making as she struggled to accommodate his shaft and the copious drool being produced pushed him even closer to coming.

In an attempt to stave off the inevitable, Lukus pulled out to give her another long breath. The long strings of drool now spilling out on her chin painted the most exquisite picture of submission for the Dom. His control was slipping. His dominance was flaring. The two fused into action. He quickly resumed fucking her mouth deeper and faster than before, setting a punishing pace. The panic was returning to her eyes and he immediately backed it off.

Dammit, Mitchell, get control. You're gonna scare the shit out of her. There's plenty of time. Slow it down.

As he resumed a slower, shallower pace, he could see annoyance had replaced fear in her eyes. For the first time, she let go of the railings to push him away.

After gasping for air, Tiff panted out at him in a huff. "Don't slow down. I trust you, Lukus."

His relief and pride surged forward. "'Sir.' When I'm face fucking you, dominating you, I'm Sir. I'll be Lukus again after I come."

Tiffany's playful grin told him she understood the rules to the game. Still, her reply was soft, tentative, as if she were trying it out to see how it sounded.

"Yes, Sir." She nailed it.

"Oh fuck, yeah. That's my girl. Now take it

deep." He didn't need to tell Tiff to hold onto the rails again. She took the submissive position naturally. He felt her anticipation of what was to come as he began to push her harder and faster, each stroke deeper and longer until she was struggling beautifully to take the punishing pace. Her eyes flared with pride as she kept up with his every thrust, meeting him stroke for stroke.

"I'm so close. I'm gonna shoot my cum deep in your throat Tiff and you're going to swallow every single drop, do you hear me? If I tell you to *show,* you'll stop swallowing and open your mouth and show me my cum that's washing your mouth, waiting to slide down your throat. I want to watch you slurp up every single drop. You think you can do that, baby?"

His answer came in the form of her attempting to answer with his dick shoved in her throat. It resulted in the most heavenly gurgling vibrations that finally pushed him over the cliff into a powerful orgasm. He let the first two strong ropes of cum spurt out, depositing them deep down her throat. It felt so good, he had to force himself to pull out slightly to place the next two spurts into her waiting, warm mouth. He could see her struggling with the load and tested her.

"Show."

For some adorable reason, Tiff decided now was when she was going to get shy. After all of the intense things they'd done together, he watched as she turned a cute shade of pink, blushing as she opened her mouth tentatively, sticking her spunk-covered tongue out slightly. There was still enough there, it was starting to drip down her chin as she held her mouth open, perfectly submissive.

Damn, she's perfect. I'm in so much trouble here.

"Swallow." After she managed to get down all in her mouth, Lukus seductively used his finger to scoop up the drops threatening to get away as they dribbled down her chin. He placed his cum-filled finger on her lips and she opened, giving him entry to deposit the remaining load in her mouth, forcing her to suck his fingers clean. Once done, she began to let go of the rails.

"Tsk, tsk. I didn't tell you to move yet, baby. You have one more important thing to do before you're done."

Letting actions speak louder than words, he leaned forward again, placing his deflating cock at her lips. "Clean me up. That's a submissive's job, to always make sure her Master's cock is cleaned off after each servicing."

Apparently, she took her role very seriously as she almost attacked his tool, pulling away briefly so she could mumble a quick, "Yes, Sir."

When she had him cleaned up, Lukus flopped down next to her, pulling her into his arms to hold her gently. "Come here, Tiff. That was absolutely amazing. Did I hurt you?"

"God, no. I got a little scared there for a few minutes, but really, I've been waiting for you to do that—*wanting* you to do it—since you tied me down in the audience pit. I was hoping you'd come back and just face-fuck me then and there when I was tied up and couldn't get away from you."

Lukus was chuckling. "You need to tell me these things. I can't read your mind."

"I don't know. You seem to be doing a pretty good job of it so far."

"Really? Good to know." Her answer pleased him. "So, you gonna tell me what you want to happen next, or want me to guess?"

Her playful chuckle reminded Lukus he was doing something with a woman he hadn't done in, well, he didn't remember. He was snuggling after having slept in on a Sunday morning, playfully bantering with an amazing, intelligent partner who just happened to be the sexiest woman he'd ever met.

A guy could get used to this.

"I think you should guess." Her voice was playful.

"Okay. Let's see. You want me to roll you over and suck on your clit until you come too?"

"Close. Even tempting, but sadly, no."

"No? You're turning down a Lukus Mitchell tongue bath?"

"When you put it that way... Wait, no. I'll take a rain check. What I really want more than anything is a trip to the bathroom to pee and brush my teeth and then some hot breakfast. I'm starving, aren't you?"

"Wow, you really are the perfect woman. You give me a mind-blowing blowjob and then you want to feed me?"

"Oh, no. I think you misunderstood. I'm the guest here. You're gonna feed *me*." She was tracing her fingers across his skin as she lay close to him, using his hard chest for her pillow. He missed seeing her expressive eyes.

"I already fed you."

"Hey, that was just an appetizer. I need the main course."

Chuckling, Lukus rolled away and finally stood. He reached back to help Tiff from the bed. They took a minute to embrace, enjoying the feel of the other's nakedness.

"Okay, you get started in there first and I'll come join you in the shower in a few minutes. I'm gonna find some clothes for us."

"You're gonna come in the bathroom with me?" He detected a quaver in her voice.

"Yeah. I can't use the guest bath since I suspect Brianna and Markus will be up soon, if they aren't already."

"But... I mean..."

Lukus reached to cup her face in his hands, making it impossible for her to look away. "Enough. I know what you're thinking, but that's the way it's going to be for us, baby. No lines. No secrets. Now go."

She looked like she might argue back, but instead surprised him with a quiet, "Yes, Sir" instead.

As she turned to head to the bathroom, Lukus deposited a quick swat on her ass, eliciting the most wonderful squeal.

Better hang on tight, Mitchell. It's a good thing you've always loved wild rides.

CHAPTER EIGHT

MARKUS

The smell of bacon and coffee were wafting through the air as Brianna and Markus finally emerged, freshly showered, from the guest room. Markus grabbed Bri's hand possessively as they made their way to the kitchen to join Lukus and Tiffany. As much as he'd have preferred to stay in bed all day with his wayward wife, the hunger in the pit of his stomach mixed with the curiosity over what had transpired between Lukus and Tiffany finally enticed him out of their bedroom. Markus didn't need to talk to his best friend to know he'd scored last night with Tiff. He'd heard them fucking loud and clear from all the way down the hall before dawn.

I hope I didn't make a mistake talking Lukus into giving Tiffany a chance. I'm gonna kick his ass if he hurts her. Not to mention, Bri is gonna kill me if she finds out I had a role to play in getting Tiff's heart broken.

The thought of a broken-hearted Tiffany evaporated as they rounded the corner and caught their first glimpse of Lukus and Tiff. Tiffany was sitting on a high-backed bar stool, legs spread as Lukus stood in front of her, pressing in tightly, one hand molded against her ass, the other cradling her neck, pulling her closer as they made out like teenagers on prom night. Only the smoke billowing out of the nearby frying pan could tear Markus's attention away from the unexpected spectacle.

"Jesus Christ. You two trying to burn down the loft?"

Lukus snapped out of their embrace to quickly rescue the burning bacon. "Fuck. I hate burnt bacon."

"And I thought you said you were a good cook. Looks like you could use a few cooking lessons." Tiffany was taunting him. Between bacon flipping, Lukus shot her a warning look that should have brought a halt to any teasing, but one flash of her bright smile had Lukus melting into his own grin.

Tiffany's playful giggle caught Markus's attention. He'd known Tiff for years and was glad to hear laughter that indicated nothing untoward had upset her, yet. Still, her mirth seemed out of place. It took Markus some time to figure out why.

Over the years, he'd been around Lukus and

dozens of his women, but never once had one looked so at home. Not only was Tiff lounging in one of Lukus's dress shirts, she was watching Lukus cook instead of actually doing it herself. She looked like she belonged here, and that in-and-of-itself was unfamiliar. But it was what she said next that almost blew his mind.

"Honey, can you pour me some more coffee? You may burn bacon, but you make a mean cup of Joe."

Honey? WTF? Lukus waiting on her? I think we've entered the Twilight Zone. *Someone swapped out Lukus with an imposter overnight.*

Markus felt Bri pull her hand away and he watched his wife rush forward to greet her best friend.

"Morning, Tiff. I'm so glad to see you're still here." Markus could see his wife's mischievous grin before she turned to address her host. "Breakfast smells wonderful. Have any coffee to spare, Lukus?"

Lukus reached for another mug, filling a coffee for Bri and delivering both steaming cups to the ladies.

"Your coffee, Mrs. Lambert." Lukus played it up with a playful bow as he served their beverage, planting a quick kiss to her cheek in the form of a welcome.

"Why thank you, kind sir." Even from his distance, Markus could see the twinkle in his wife's eyes as she bantered with Lukus. A twinge of jealousy hit him, but he immediately squashed it down as he replayed a vision of their time on the stage the night before. Had Bri flashed one of her flirty smiles at any other man, Markus would have dropped them on the spot, but if the last forty-eight hours had taught him anything, he'd learned his wife really did love him, and his best friend was loyal to a fault.

Still he couldn't resist joining the fun. "Wow, Mitchell. I didn't know you were moonlighting as a short-order cook and waiter. I'll take a steak and eggs. Over easy."

"Smart ass. Make yourself useful and mix me up a Bloody Mary."

"Hey. You never offered me a Bloody Mary." Tiff's impish pout caught Lukus's attention and having properly rescued the bacon, he moved back to stand close enough to Tiff for her to wrap her arms around his neck and pull him closer.

"I need to keep you sober, baby. I don't want you to say I got you drunk and took advantage of you." His roguish smile made it clear he was having fun.

Markus had to think back pretty far to recall the last time he'd seen his best friend looking this happy and relaxed. Granted, the last few years had been fraught with plenty of stress in their friendship. Between the whole Georgie debacle and the now settled lawsuit hanging over Lukus's head, there'd been more bad than good shadowing their relationship. Markus wondered if Lukus was feeling the same lifting of the black cloud he was.

As if finding out Bri wants to explore a D/s relationship isn't amazing enough, it feels damn good to have my brother *back.*

With that thought, a memory of a similarly happy Lukus came to mind. It had been years earlier on the day they'd taken a road-trip to Indiana to pay a visit to a mutual Dom friend of theirs who specialized in making top-notch punishment and restraint devices such as spanking benches, stocks, and St. Andrew's crosses. Lukus had been outfitting his new club at the time and was on cloud nine, as he was about to realize a long-time dream. The fact Markus saw the same level of happiness on his friend's face this morning told him maybe he'd been worrying about the wrong friend's heart getting broken.

While Lukus, Tiffany, and Brianna bantered easily, Markus moved across the room to the bar, in part to mix up a pitcher of Bloody Marys, but more importantly, to give himself some time to think through the long-term implications of this weekend's events. Without a doubt, he knew his life had changed at the most basic level. In a moment of clarity, he realized the four friends would forevermore view life as *before that weekend* and *after that weekend.*

Having completed his bartending duties, Markus crossed back to the kitchen with a large pitcher of breakfast cocktails in tow. "So who wants a Bloody Mary?"

Three people answered in unison as if they'd practiced. "I do."

Lukus had put Brianna to work chopping veggies for what looked like a planned omelet. Tiff jumped down from her perch to meet Markus at the cabinet housing the glassware.

"Let me help you with the glasses, Markus."

Their fingers brushed as Tiffany handed him the first glass. Markus took the opportunity to hold her hand in his, forcing Tiff to turn her attention up to him. Her shining eyes told him what he needed to know, yet he still had to ask.

"Is everything okay this morning, Tiff?"

He could see the warmth in her expression deepen as she responded quietly. "Thanks for asking Markus, but everything is absolutely perfect this morning."

He could feel the grin playing at his lips. "Perfect, you say?"

"Yep. Perfect."

"Well, that's a good thing because I'd hate to have to kick his ass if he hurt you."

A mischievous smile he'd never seen there before adorned Tiff's face, enhanced by her adorable pink blush. "Hurt me? Well, it wasn't anything I couldn't handle."

Markus chuckled. "That wasn't necessarily the

only kind of hurt I was worried about, Tiff, but it's good to know."

Markus almost lost his grip on the pitcher as Lukus shoved him aside to pull Tiffany into his arms. "I don't appreciate you trying to move in on my girl, Markus."

Tiffany molded herself to Lukus as she replied. "I like the sound of that... *my girl*. Markus was just trying to make sure you were taking good care of *your girl,* is all."

"Ah, so he doesn't trust me, is that it?"

Markus grabbed the glass out of Tiff's hand and started to pour.

"Give it a rest, Lukus."

He handed the adult beverage to his best friend before reaching for the next glass and filling it for Tiff. Once all four of them had their drinks, Markus moved to Brianna to wrap his arm intimately around her waist before raising his glass to offer up a toast.

"To one hell of a weekend. I'm not sure about all of you, but I get the feeling life is never gonna be the same as it was when we all woke up Friday morning."

His eye caught with Lukus and the best friends shared a silent exchange that spoke volumes. All four of them moved closer to clink their glasses in a salute to the life-changing weekend before quietly sipping their drinks.

Brianna spoke first. "Honey, Lukus may be a

good short-order cook, but I think you missed your calling as a bartender. The only thing missing is the celery."

Setting his drink down on the counter, Markus pulled his wife into his arms. "I made them pretty strong. I'm hoping to get you drunk so I can take you home and have my way with you."

Brianna flirted in return. "Honey, you don't need to get me drunk to have your way with me. I thought we already established I'm all yours. You can have your way with me any time you want."

Markus tested her. "Really? How about right now?"

He could see the surprise cross her face, then lust. She was tempted. "Okay. Let's go back to the bedroom."

"Nope. Here. Now."

It was quiet enough to hear a pin drop as all four of them stood silently, all eyes on Brianna, waiting to see how she'd react to their new reality. Markus briefly felt guilty for testing her before they'd even had a chance to talk about what the introduction of BDSM into their marriage was really going to mean to each of them. Still, he was curious to see how deep her submissive desires ran. But he was suddenly conflicted, not even sure himself what he was hoping for. Brianna didn't let her gaze waver from his own.

With a confident smile, Brianna finally answered him. "I'd rather not, Sir. I will if it's that important to you Markus, but I'd rather keep the changes in our marriage private. Please."

The surprised relief he felt gave Markus his own answer. "Good girl. I was hoping you might feel that way. I'll reward you later."

Brianna licked her lips, looking like she might regret her decision. "You could reward me now, in the bedroom, if you'd like."

He couldn't help but chuckle. "Oh I like the idea of making you wait better. Now, get back to making that omelet. I think we're all ready to eat."

"Yes, Sir." Her face broke out in a brilliant smile that warmed his heart.

Tiffany

They were just about to sit down to eat when Tiffany heard the ding of the arriving elevator. She looked up to see the towering Derek emerge with his petite wife following a few steps behind. Tiff was relieved to see Rachel was at least dressed this morning, although the tiny plaid mini-skirt and white button-down midriff blouse left little to the imagination. Only when Tiff caught a glimpse of her knee-high stockings and saddle shoes did she put together Rachel was playing the role of the naughty schoolgirl this morning, pigtails and all.

As Derek moved closer to the kitchen, Tiff glimpsed the wide leather Irish school strap hanging on a hook from his even wider leather belt. A pussy-warming flashback smacked her hard at the sight of the dreaded strap. She had to close her eyes to try to catch her breath.

She tried valiantly to think of something—anything—that could take her mind off the unexpected invasion of memories of her earliest sexual stirrings as a teenager. She'd been an impressionable young woman growing up in a strict Catholic community where corporal punishment was a way of life. She might have had a chance to clear her mind in some other situation, but sitting here, surrounded by the aura of a dominant Lukus and two couples who looked like they could drop to the floor to fuck each other's brains out at a moment's notice, Tiff found it hard to force her mind to dwell on more mundane memories.

After managing to slow her breathing as best she could, Tiff finally opened her eyes to find Lukus had silently moved directly in front of her. His dark green eyes were watching her intently. Of course, he would have picked up on the subtle changes in her since Derek and Rachel's arrival. He didn't beat around the bush.

"What's wrong?" At least he asked quietly.

Not wanting to draw any more attention to herself than she already had, Tiff impatiently tried to shush him. "Nothing. Let's eat."

The concern in Lukus' eyes was immediately replaced with anger. Without taking his eyes away from Tiffany's, he addressed the group. "We'll be right back. You guys eat without us. Tiffany and I have something we need to discuss. In private."

When he grabbed her hand to pull her along with him, panic took over and she dug in, refusing to move her feet. Undeterred, Lukus lifted her effortlessly in his arms, eliciting a squeal from Tiff as he quickly relocated them to his bedroom. He managed to slam the door closed with a loud kick before dropping Tiff on the bed, quickly trapping her beneath him as he caged her in, his feet firmly planted on the ground.

"I think I made it clear what would happen if you lied to me, didn't I?"

On a scale of one to ten, her heart rate skyrocketed to eleven. "I didn't lie. I don't know what you're so upset about, Lukus."

"Don't you? Your entire body language changed the second Derek and Rachel arrived, so don't you dare tell me it's nothing."

She was smart enough to know not to say it again. "I don't want to talk about it... especially not out there with everyone else around."

"Then what should your answer have been?"

They were in one of their staring showdowns. No surprise—she lost. "I guess I could have said I just didn't want to talk about it right then."

"Yes. Or we'd talk about it later, in private."

"Fine. We'll talk about it later, in private."

Lukus's smile was predatory. "Lucky you. We're in private now. What happened when Derek and Rachel came in?"

"I don't want to talk about it yet."

"Too fucking bad. I want to know what's going through your pretty head."

Tiffany's breathing was getting raspy again. "Please... I..." She could feel the heat rising in her face.

Lukus's face was lighting up. "You're adorable when you blush."

Sassy Tiffany flared. "So glad you approve of my discomfort, ya big jerk." She tried, unsuccessfully, to push him away from her so she could sit up.

Tiff wasn't sure how it happened so fast, but the next thing she knew, she was face down over Lukus's lap as he sat on the side of the bed. Her long-flowing blond hair was the only part of her body touching the floor. The feel of his first swat with his strong right hand surprised her more than it actually hurt, but by the third strong spank, the reality of what was happening was sinking in. The dress shirt she was wearing had risen up and the thin material of the borrowed boxer briefs underneath gave her little in the way of protection from Lukus's punishment.

It only took about ten seconds for her anger to be replaced with submissive emotions. The memories she'd thought of in the kitchen, of watching her best friend's twin sister being punished by her boyfriend with the dreaded Irish school strap, flickered through her consciousness as Lukus continued to deliver open-handed swats in a fast volley. Tiff was pretty sure he was holding back from using his full strength, but it didn't take long for the heat to build up enough that she was squirming to get away.

When she lifted her right hand back to try to protect her ass, Lukus effortlessly snatched it, restraining it behind her back without so much as missing a beat. It felt odd to be holding his hand, their fingers intimately entwined, while he lit up her ass with his other punishing hand.

When he stopped about a minute later, she was grateful. She'd clamped her lips tight to keep from calling out to him as the pain got to the point where she wasn't sure she'd be able to maintain her composure. When she felt him pulling the boxer briefs down to expose her most-likely pink butt, she finally lost it. "Oh, no! Please, no more! I'm sorry!"

Continuing on with the spanking, Lukus answered her. "Yes, I bet you're sorry now. I didn't think I was getting through to you, but I might have your attention now."

"Oh yes, you do! Please, Lukus! That's enough! Oweeee!"

She may have been begging him to stop, but even in her duress, she could feel the wetness pooling at her core. Each time his hand connected with her bottom she could feel her pussy pulsing. It was both pleasure and pain at its finest.

The steady spanking continued without interruption as Lukus began to lecture her.

"Time for more ground rules, baby. Rule number one. During a punishment, I decide when you've had enough. I promised you a safe word and you'll have one for play, but the only word you get during a punishment is *yellow*. It will get you a short break and I'll evaluate, but your punishment ends when I decide you've learned your lesson. Not before."

"Oh Lukus. I have. Please....!" Tiff could feel the tears pooling as she tried valiantly not to dissolve into a sobbing mess.

"Rule number two. I'm always 'Sir' during a punishment. No exceptions." He made his point with a few especially strong spanks to her tender sit-spot.

"Ohhhhh. I'm sorry, Sir."

His dominance melted her core. The sound of his hand as it soundly connected with her bare bottom stirred her most primal inner need. Before this very minute, she'd worried her independent streak might have decided to rear its head in the face of a punishment, making her questionable submissive material. It'd been one of her hidden concerns about making the journey from voyeur to submissive. But as her tears began in earnest, she realized she'd worried for nothing. The truth was becoming clearer with each passing moment of her first real punishment.

All these years. I've been waiting... dreaming of this... dreaming of him.

Rather than panic in the face of the pain, Tiffany instead acknowledged the relief of finding a man who was finally going to be strong enough to guide and protect her. She couldn't help but be relieved he was already so tuned into her that he could notice even small nuances in her mood. The fact she could feel his growing erection under her tummy was icing on the cake.

"Now, tell me why you're getting this beautiful ass of yours spanked."

"I don't know!"

Several strong swats later he prompted again. "Want to try your answer again?"

Through her tears she apologized. "Please... I'm sorry."

"Sorry for what, baby?"

"Being sassy and calling you a jerk," Tiff choked out.

Lukus finished the swat already in progress, but finally halted the spanking, leaving her upside down. Tiff was relieved he'd stopped, but was more than aware of the vision she must have made for Lukus right now, her pink ass in the air ready for more punishment if she misbehaved again. The memories that had started this whole chain of events returned with a vengeance and she was happy he couldn't see her face in this precarious position.

Lukus was still holding her right hand in his own as he gently began to massage her thighs, careful to avoid rubbing relief to her burning ass. "Now that we have that cleared up, I think I'll leave you in this position as we go back to the beginning of our conversation. That way, if I don't like your answers, I'm ready to pick up where I left off. I'll ask one more time. What was wrong when Derek and Rachel arrived? Don't try to tell me nothing because I saw it. Something upset you and I want to know what it was. Are you afraid of Derek?"

Tiffany was glad he added on the last question. That was an easy one to answer. "I'm not afraid of Derek, no. I know you'd never let him hurt me."

"Damn straight. I'm the only one who's going to be touching this beautiful body of yours. So, if not Derek, what had you spooked?"

It may have been only a day since she'd met him, but Tiff had already learned there was no point in trying to hide anything from this remarkable man. She had no idea how, but he'd know if she held anything back. Total truth was the only path forward.

"It was Rachel dressed as a naughty schoolgirl. That and Derek carrying the Irish school strap on his belt. It looks exactly like the strap my high school friends always had hanging in the dining room at their house. Her parents were very strict and would use it to punish Mary Ellen and her brothers and sisters if they got in trouble."

"I see. Were they punished in front of you, or after you'd left, and you just heard about it from Mary Ellen?"

"Oh, God. Don't make me talk about this. Please."

"Answer me, baby. How else are we going to learn more about each other?" His words were a command, but his tone was soft, patient.

"Both." Her reply came out in a whimper.

"Tell me. Were you ever a naughty girl who had to be punished while at their house?"

With a relieved whoosh Tiff answered truthfully. "Oh, no. I was terrified it might happen, though. I was so careful to never do anything that might get me in trouble while I was there."

"Interesting. Were you that afraid of a spanking, Tiff?" His voice sounded wary, as if he might have already pushed her too hard.

She wasn't sure she knew how to explain it. "Not exactly."

"So what exactly?"

"I was more afraid of embarrassing myself in front of Mary Ellen and her family."

"I see. So, the humiliation of the public punishment would be worse than the punishment itself?"

"Sort of."

"Explain."

"Please, Sir. Can we talk about this later?"

Tiff should have kept her mouth shut. At least over his knee he couldn't see her expressions. As if knowing he was at a disadvantage by not seeing her eyes, he helped her stand before immediately pulling her to sit in his lap, the borrowed boxers still bunched at her knees as she rested on her tender red cheeks. He took the time to brush her now messy hair back from her face, swiping gently at the stray tears he'd caused with his punishment.

Lukus flashed her a supportive smile after getting her cleaned up. "We'll talk about it now, Tiff. These are important things for us to discuss. There's nothing about you I don't want to know." Cupping her face gently with the same hand that had moments ago been connecting with her bottom, Lukus let her calm further before pushing again. "Answer me, please. Were you more afraid of the pain of the punishment or of being embarrassed by being punished in front of your friend?"

"Neither, I guess."

Lukus looked mildly surprised. "Okay. I didn't expect that answer. Keep going, baby."

"I just didn't want what happened to Mary Ellen's twin sister to happen to me. I would have just died." Tiff could feel her breathing coming heavy again.

"I'll bite. What happened to Mary Ellen's sister?"

"Let's just say Kathleen was a brat. By the time we were ready to leave for college, she was getting a strapping at least once a week for one reason or another."

"Let me guess. Kathleen liked it. She was probably a budding submissive."

"Oh, yeah. I'm pretty sure she was an exhibitionist, too. She loved the attention being in trouble would bring her. Mary Ellen would joke that she could predict Kathleen's mood and behavior based on who else was visiting. She would do something to earn a spanking more often when I was there, but she would pull out all the stops when other friends came over."

"Let me guess. When her brother's friends came over?"

"How'd you know that?"

Lukus was chuckling. "Lucky guess."

"I'd never seen anything like it. I would have been mortified if I were her, but it was like she enjoyed having an audience. I think her parents figured out what was going on, too, because at that point she was only strapped in private. But we were all just in the next room so we could still hear everything. She was very... vocal. There were times I would have rather been in the room watching than in the kitchen with the rest of the family."

"You liked to watch?"

"No... well, yes. I mean... stop getting me confused."

Lukus was full-out laughing at her now. "Oh, baby. I'm gonna say it again, but I'd refrain from calling me a big jerk if I were you. You're adorable when you blush."

Tiffany bit her lower lip. She really did want to call him a jerk again, but her ass talked her into holding back. "Gee... thanks."

"So why not the kitchen?"

"It was worse being in the next room with her brothers and their friends. If their mom was there it was bad enough, but when their mom wasn't in the kitchen... let's just say I learned a lot about sex in that kitchen listening as Kathleen got her ass whipped."

"I can imagine. Teenage boys would have a field day with something like that."

"Well, and by the time this was happening, we were all in college. They all knew their sister had gotten off on getting strapped and talked about wanting to find women like her in college. I knew her brothers really well because I would practice basketball drills and play one-on-one with them. I was so worried that... well... I just tried to melt into the background, hoping they'd never notice what happened when I thought of being spanked with that damn strap."

"I think I'm starting to understand. You were most afraid that her brothers would notice that you were getting turned on by the spanking, weren't you?"

Tiffany nodded.

"They were all home on a college break when her brother David brought his roommate, John, home for the weekend. Kathleen outdid herself that time. She wrecked her car talking on her cell phone. I'd never seen her parents so mad. They hauled her out of the room and we could hear her upstairs, wailing. Well, her brothers were having a field day making fun of her in the kitchen, but I noticed John just sat there very quiet... serious... listening carefully. After a few minutes, he yelled at the guys to knock it off or he'd kick their asses. I couldn't believe they all just shut up. It was almost like they were afraid of him or something."

"Ahh. John was a budding Dom."

Tiffany pondered before answering. "I never thought of it like that, but you're surely right because it wasn't long before Kathleen started dating John. He'd come home from college almost every weekend to see her. The change in her was remarkable. She stopped being bratty almost immediately. At first, I didn't have a clue why."

"Let me guess. John took control of her. He knew what she needed to keep her reined in and behaving."

Tiffany looked into the deep green eyes of Lukus, totally in awe of his intuitive read of the situation. "Of course, you'd figure that out, Mr. Dom." Tiffany didn't care for the smug smile that lit up his face. "I better be careful. I'm giving you a big head."

Lukus's smile turned merry. "Oh, baby. You do like to flirt with fire, don't you? I'd keep going with your story if I were you before you find yourself over my lap again."

"For the record, I hate that you can tell there's more to the story," she teased.

When she delayed, he urged her on. "Keep going."

Tiffany was getting alarmed. Not that she practiced lying, but if she stuck with Lukus, she could see she was not going to be able to get away with hiding anything from him.

Who am I kidding? There is no 'if.' There's no way I'm walking away from this amazing man.

With a frustrated sigh, Tiff continued on. "It was just before I was going to be leaving for college. I'd been so busy practicing basketball and the pressure of the scholarship and leaving home was closing in. Going over to Mary Ellen's was like my only safe haven where I could get away from the stress that was building. We'd spend hours hanging out in the big treehouse they had in their backyard, listening to music and reading. It had been her brothers' hangout, but as they got older, we girls had taken over. We'd sneak out there to... well... damn." After stopping to throw in a flirty smile, she continued on. "It feels like I'm confessing something to my father instead of my boyfriend all of a sudden. Anyway, I don't even remember how, but we'd somehow got our hands on several racy romance novels and *Cosmo* magazines. Mary Ellen even found a couple back copies of *Penthouse Forums* under her brother's mattress. We would sneak out to the treehouse to read our contraband."

"You *were* a naughty girl. Did you get caught and strapped?"

Tiff was relieved he'd finally guessed wrong. "Wrong, mister know-it-all."

She caught the flash in his eyes and knew she was pushing him too far. Tiff quickly plunged forward with the rest of the story to avoid giving him time to turn her back over his knee.

"When we heard people coming up the ladder, I about had a heart attack. We quickly threw everything into our hiding place and then hid behind the big couch. Only when the door slammed and we heard John admonishing Kathleen for being a naughty girl did we know it wasn't one of Mary Ellen's parents who'd come in. I wanted to just stand up and tell them we were there, but Mary Ellen held me down and shushed me to keep us hidden. I still can't believe we hid there for almost an hour."

Lukus's eyes were turning dark again. "I'm guessing my little voyeur heard a bit more than she bargained for."

"Oh, yes. Heard and saw. For an impressionable eighteen-year-old virgin, it was an education to be sure. I couldn't believe he had her dressed in her school uniform, even though school was long over. He pulled her over his lap and then he pulled her panties down to her knees... and... he spanked her bare ass really hard with her dad's strap until even I could tell she was so close to coming, but all of a sudden he just stopped and... well..."

Lukus waited patiently for her to proceed.

"He tied her hands behind her back with a scarf and then had her kneel at his feet and give him a blowjob. I'd never seen anything like it. The rougher he got with her, the more she seemed to like it until he eventually came in her mouth and made her swallow. Then he had her lie over his lap like she had when she was getting strapped and he finger fucked her while calling her a naughty little slut until she came all over his hand. I swear I actually came in my panties that day just listening and watching her get her punishment and reward."

"Such a naughty little voyeur."

"Well, I wasn't the only one. As you can imagine, things got kinda weird between Mary Ellen and me after that. As guilty as I felt about coming while I watched, I know she felt even worse because I'd caught her playing with herself as she listened, too. She was mortified at getting turned on by listening to her sister like that. Luckily, I left for college not long after and that's when I met Brianna. It took a long time at college before I started to read and better understand why my body had reacted the way it had. I didn't know it at the time, but watching those early corporal punishments set a foundation for why I was attracted to the whole BDSM lifestyle in the first place."

"Well I'm glad you shared this. How else am I gonna know how far I can push you, what you're going to like, and what will just upset you?"

Tiff snuggled against his chest, in part to get closer to him, but in part to avoid looking into his probing eyes.

"I know you're right, Lukus. I just didn't think we had to tell everything so fast."

"It'll come out as it needs to, baby. I couldn't ignore the look on your face when you saw Derek and Rachel come in."

"All it took was one look at them and I couldn't stop the flashbacks from coming. It just happened so fast. Can't we please just go back out there and forget about all of this for a while?"

He didn't answer right away and when he did, she could hear a new strain in his voice. "You're right. I've been pushing you hard. Maybe we're moving too fast."

Tiffany didn't like hearing uncertainty in Lukus's voice. She'd thought she wanted to slow things down, but hearing him say it, she knew that wasn't what she wanted at all.

I want him so bad, it hurts. If that means going full-steam ahead, then so be it.'

"Lukus, I'm fine. Really. I just overreacted."

"No, you're right to feel rushed. I mean, we've barely just met."

She tried not to panic, having no clue what she should say. She was grateful he filled the silence.

"How is this beautiful ass of yours?" She loved the feel of his tender caress across her exposed backside.

Desperate to regain their intimacy, she burrowed even closer into his neck. "It's properly punished, Sir."

"And... how is this pussy of yours? Open up for me. Inspection time."

With an embarrassed groan, Tiffany opened her legs slightly, allowing Lukus to push his probing fingers into her sopping wet pussy.

"Oh baby, I think you were enjoying your time over my knee and taking your trip down memory lane. What are we going to do with you?"

Tiffany didn't answer him with words. Her body was doing a fine job of answering for her. She opened her legs wider, allowing her body to hump against his hand, looking for enough precious friction to get her the relief she was looking for.

Lukus's mouth closed in on hers as he plunged several fingers deep into her pussy, finding her G-spot almost instantly. It literally took him less than a minute to bring her to climax with nothing more than a probing tongue and fingers.

Tiff grabbed his shirt, pulling them as close as possible as she came all over his hand. "Oh, yes. Lukus!"

"That's my naughty girl. Come again for me."

Tiffany shuddered through her orgasm before once again snuggling tightly against him to recover. If she hadn't just come so powerfully, she might have come again at the sight of Lukus bringing his cum-covered fingers to his mouth to lick them clean.

"Absolutely delicious."

"Oh. My. Freaking. God."

"Let's get you put back together and out there for some food before Derek eats it all. You've never met anyone who can eat as much as he can."

Tiff was giggling as she stood on her wobbly legs while Lukus helped her get the boxer briefs back on again. They headed back out to the kitchen hand in hand. Tiff felt a huge relief lifted from her shoulders because now she knew once and for all she hadn't just been dreaming of something she could never have.

CHAPTER NINE

BRIANNA

B rianna wasn't paying any attention to the men's conversation at the table. She was too worried about Tiffany and too mad at Markus to even think about eating. It was bad enough that Lukus had looked like a caveman hauling her best friend off to do God-knows-what, but Bri was sure she heard the rhythmic sounds of a spanking coming from the bedroom. She may not have known the why, but she knew damn well Tiffany's voyeur days were now over and Brianna couldn't help but be anxious to know if her friend was alright. When she'd attempted to go back to intervene, Markus had stopped her in her tracks with a quick swat to her already tender bottom. He'd even threatened to turn her over his knee if she didn't sit back down and stay out of it.

It's just as well. I don't have a clue what I

would have done if I'd burst into the room anyway. My luck, I'd have ended up with a punishment too.

Now Bri was forced to sit here not-so-patiently waiting for Lukus and Tiffany to return to brunch. At least the sounds of the spanking had stopped.

Rachel snapped her out of her train of thought with a quiet reassurance. "She'll be fine with Master Lukus. He'll never hurt her. Well, not really." Her knowing smile confirmed she'd heard the spanking as well.

Brianna blushed when she realized how rude she'd been by basically ignoring Rachel. "Oh gosh. I'm so sorry. I've been a bit distracted. How rude of me."

"Oh, don't worry about me. I can just tell you're worried, and you don't need to be."

Brianna took a deep breath as she contemplated Rachel's helpful words. She remembered how even when Lukus was punishing her, she'd always known at her core he wouldn't really hurt her. Not the way Jake had. She was comforted by her revelation.

"Thank you, Rachel, for reminding me. You're right. I'm sure he knows what he's doing."

"Oh, I'm sure he does. You should have some bacon before Master Derek eats it all."

She was passing the plate of bacon when Derek piped in, a grin on his face. "I heard that, little girl."

Instead of looking worried, Rachel flashed a flirty smile at her husband and a surprised feeling of relief hit Brianna. It finally dawned on her she was relieved that even Derek and Rachel, whose relationship was pretty far to the hard-core end of the BDSM continuum, could still tease each other. Bri was still trying to figure out this whole new layer in her marriage and a small part of her had worried she'd never again be able to tease her husband for fear of a punishment.

Bri could sense his eyes on her. She glanced up to see Markus watching her from across the breakfast bar. As if sensing her unease, he flaunted one of his sexiest smiles to reassure her he was still the same man she married—just an enhanced, upgraded version. The warmth spreading across her bottom as she sat on the hard kitchen barstool was her proof the changes hadn't just been a dream. The remaining tingle from his private punishment was an intimate connection, secretly linking them.

It was with great relief when Bri looked up to see Lukus and Tiffany rejoining the group, particularly since Lukus had his arm possessively draped across Tiffany's shoulder. Tiffany had the serene look of a sated woman, and Bri knew she'd worried about nothing. In fact, she hasn't seen Tiff ever looking quite this happy.

You go, girl. It's about time you found your own someone special.

Once Lukus and Tiffany returned to their seats around the breakfast island, the group fell into an easy cadence of fun bantering over food and drinks. The pitcher of Bloody Marys was free-flowing and Brianna was feeling tipsy in no time.

Rachel pouted. "It's not fair. I don't even like to drink alcohol very often, but now that I can't, it just seems restrictive. Can I have just a taste, Sir?"

Derek's disapproval was swift. "Only if you don't want to sit down on that beautiful ass of yours for a week. Absolutely not one drop of alcohol, little girl. Not until after the baby comes."

Rachel could win an Academy Award for her performance of a naughty schoolgirl. Bri suspected her pouting was all part of the game that she and her dominant husband played as the petite brunette stomped her foot and crossed her arms across her chest in an exaggerated temper tantrum.

"That's not fair, Daddy. Everyone else gets to drink but me. I'm the only one who has to miss out."

"One more word from you and you'll also be the only one getting a strapping over my knee. Add ten more to your count for your bedtime spanking. You better slow it down. You're already up to twenty-five, and it's not even noon yet. Now drink your milk like a good little girl."

"Daaaadddddyyyyy."

She may have been calling Derek her daddy, but the look on Rachel's face was completely non-familial. In fact, it was more along the lines of feral lust. Most people may not have understood why

Rachel was purposefully antagonizing her husband when it was clear her actions were going to lead to a strapping, but knowing firsthand the pleasure she got from a punishment helped Brianna understand the dynamics at play. She may not have seen herself dressing up as a naughty schoolgirl, but she suspected she just might have been antagonizing Markus in order to get her own bottom disciplined in the very near future.

Tiff stepped in as if to defuse the situation. "It's okay, Rachel. I'll drink your share for you today." She was reaching for the almost empty pitcher when Lukus stopped her with his hand on hers.

"Absolutely not. You've had enough, baby."

Bri almost choked on her own drink as she watched Tiffany's face.

"Are you kidding me? I only had one. I think I know when I've had enough."

The room was silent as they all waited to see how this showdown of wills was going to play out. Bri was putting her money on Lukus. His dark green eyes were stormy.

"Tiffany Lauren O'Sullivan. You're going to be driving soon. You put one more drop in your mouth and I'll be borrowing Derek's strap." Lightening the mood, he swung his glare at Brianna. "Maybe Brianna would like to get sassy again too and we can watch all three of you girls get your asses lit up this morning." His smirk was annoyingly charming.

Bri grinned back. "I think I'll pass, thank you."

"Wise choice."

Derek settled the debate on the Bloody Marys by polishing off the end of the pitcher as the conversation turned to the coming week.

"So Markus, what are you going to do with all your free time now that the lawsuit is settled?"

Markus put on his all-business look. "Oh, I have a few other clients besides you two hoodlums. In fact, I'm gonna need to fly to New York for a few days mid-week. A judge out there's gotten himself in a bit of hot water and seems to think I'm the man to get him out." Turning to Brianna he continued. "I got the call on Friday and was going to talk to you about it over the weekend. Now it's more important than ever you come with me. I don't want us apart, not even for a few days, sweetheart."

Brianna's heart swelled at the look of love on her husband's face. "Honey, I'd really love to go, but I need to be here for the salon. I'm sure Tiffany and Lukus are gonna want to spend a lot of time together this week, too, and one of us needs to be here to open and close."

Before Markus could reply, Lukus surprised them all. "It's okay, Brianna. I think it's actually a good idea for you to go with Markus. Tiffany and I were just talking about how fast things are moving. I think she could use a few days to get her head wrapped around everything that's happened this weekend before we see each other again. I was going to suggest we get together next weekend anyway, so you should go with Markus to New York."

Brianna could see the disappointment on her best friend's face as she took in his words. She would have kicked Lukus under the table if the island cabinets weren't between them.

Doesn't he know how fragile Tiff is going to be feeling after this weekend? Damn him.

"I'm not sure that's such a good idea, Lukus. You and Tiff have a lot to learn about each other. I think you should spend as much time together this week as possible." Bri tried to steer him in a different direction.

"That's enough. I know what I'm doing, Brianna."

She detected his irritation, but she was not sure it was directed at her this time as she watched Tiffany and Lukus exchange a knowing look.

"I'll call Tiffany later in the week and we can see each other when you two get back into town," Lukus said.

Markus jumped in. "We'll be back by Thursday night or Friday at the latest. Right now, I think we should get cleaning up so we can head home."

Everyone else may have missed it, but Bri caught the panicked look in Tiffany's eyes. The friends shared a moment of silent communication that told Brianna how afraid Tiffany was that this weekend was just a one-night stand for Lukus and that he was going to forget about her the second she drove away. Bri shot her a supportive smile meant to reassure her that Lukus wasn't that cruel.

Lukus had obviously caught the look on Tiffany's face too because he'd moved behind her, hugging her from behind, leaning in close to whisper something that made her blush bright red before leaning in to kiss her behind her ear intimately.

All too quickly the kitchen was cleaned up and Markus was pushing to get on the road. Brianna was anxious to get home to spend more time with her husband, but she was torn. She knew each minute that brought them closer to leaving was also one minute closer to when Tiffany would need to walk away from Lukus, even if only for a few days.

Tiff had already changed back into her dress from the day before. Brianna managed to get a few minutes alone with Lukus while everyone else said their good-byes. He took her hands in his as they looked into each other's eyes. She was quickly overwhelmed with gratitude for this remarkable man. Unexpected tears clouded her vision as Lukus wrapped her in his arms, pulling her close against his muscular chest. She hugged him tightly as the tears began to fall in earnest.

"Shhhh. There's no need for tears, sweetheart."

"Yes, there is. I can't thank you enough, Lukus, for all you've done for Markus and me this weekend. I know how lucky I am to be going home with my husband today. Things could have turned out so very differently."

"I'm not sure I'd call it luck. You're one stubborn woman. Don't forget all you went through to avoid signing the damn divorce papers. I sure as hell hope you've learned your lesson." She couldn't see his eyes, but she could hear the warning in his voice and knew he was not joking.

"Without a doubt, Sir." They pulled out of their hug in time for Bri to see the satisfied smile on Lukus's face at her response.

"You'd better be a good girl. You know Markus is a charter member of the club. He's welcome back any time he has need of our services." The twinkle in Lukus's eye was the only thing keeping Brianna's heart rate from skyrocketing. He may have been telling the truth, but she also knew he was teasing.

"Hopefully, next time we come, it'll just be for a fun visit."

Lukus's smile turned naughty before pulling her into his embrace one more time. "You're welcome to come for a fun visit anytime. In fact, I can't wait to see what your definition of fun is, Bri."

His warm chuckle warmed her heart as he pulled back to watch her reaction.

Brianna couldn't resist. "Well, I was hoping to get a front row seat to watch Tiffany beat you at basketball. I heard she did a pretty good job of that once already."

The look on his face was priceless. Bri worried

she pushed him too far, but he eventually broke into a broad smile. "She really is fucking amazing, isn't she?"

She caught him glancing over at Tiff, with an unbridled look of passion. It was the same look she found on her husband's face as he stared at her from across the room.

Never in her wildest dreams could Brianna have predicted how things would turn out this weekend when she woke up on Friday morning. She had always known she was lucky, but now she knew she got to have it all.

Lukus

A knot formed in his chest as Lukus saw Derek driving down the alley with Tiffany's car. He knew how irrational his reaction was, yet he couldn't shake the feeling he was about to let something special come to an end. Of course, he knew they'd see each other again and they'd talk, but Lukus was suddenly struck by a fear that there'd been a powerful universal force at work this weekend. The stars had aligned to bring Brianna and Markus together, better and stronger than they had been before. A miraculous force had to be at work to turn Derek and Rachel into parents, setting their lives on a new and exciting course.

Those were important feats all by themselves, but it was the mysterious, powerful force that had delivered Tiffany to his doorstep that the Dom thought of now as they stood holding hands, each feeling the seconds ticking by that would mark her departure. Fear gripped him that the magic bubble surrounding them would burst as soon as she drove away.

Knock it off. You're being a total pussy, Mitchell. You have work to do today and you both need some distance to get some perspective on the last forty-eight hours. Put her in her car and watch her drive away. You'll talk to her in a few days.

Derek stopped right in front of them, pulling up directly behind Markus's Porsche. Markus and Bri were already loaded and ready to go, waiting on Tiff to say goodbye.

After getting out from behind the wheel, Derek stepped forward to capture Tiffany in a bear hug, squeezing her in his massive arms. He almost swallowed her up, causing Lukus to step forward.

"Hey, what the fuck man? Let go of my girl."

Derek finally released her and stepped away, a shit-eating grin on his face. "You have no idea how much fun it is to yank your chain, do you man?"

Derek turned his attention back to Tiff. "It was great to meet you Tiffany. I'll look forward to seeing a lot more of you around here 'cause I have a feeling he's gonna be a real bear to deal with when he hasn't seen you for a few days. Don't be a stranger."

Tiffany looked pleased with Derek's sentiment. "Thanks Derek. It was great to meet you and Rachel. I hope I see you both around, too."

Lukus had had enough of the mutual love-fest. Despite wanting to haul her back upstairs to his loft, he shuffled her towards the open car door, determined to not be a pussy. She turned back to him rather than taking a seat behind the wheel. Her look was expectant, hopeful.

"So, I guess this is it. We're gonna slow things down I know, but I really will be waiting for your call later in the week, Lukus. I mean..." Her voice trailed off. He knew she was fighting their go-slow plan in her pretty little head. He'd have to be strong for both of them.

"I promise you, Tiff, unless I get run over by a bus and am in the hospital, I'm going to call you Wednesday night and we'll make plans to see each other again. This wasn't a one-night stand for me. I just want to make sure you have the time you need to process all of this before we get back together again."

"I know you think you're slowing down for me, but I don't need to go slow, Lukus. If you want to wait for a few days, that's fine. We'll wait. But don't try to pass it off that you're doing it for me. I just want you to be truthful with yourself is all."

Lukus had no response. He was completely conflicted between wanting to caution her that she needed to trust his decision to know what was best for them and not wanting to have the last words he said to her before she drove away to be disciplinary. He was also realizing she might have been onto something. The closer he got to having to say goodbye, the more he knew it was going to gut him to be away from her for days.

He stood there paralyzed, weighing his options. He was no longer debating with Tiffany. The debate had turned internal. One side of him wanted to scoop her up and carry her back upstairs, to hold her hostage in his bedroom. The other side of him was ready to let her drive away because that seemed easier than taking back his earlier decision.

I'm her Dom, damn it. I make command decisions and I stick with them. We'll wait to talk until Wednesday.

Lukus reached out to pull her into his arms, planting one last, long kiss on her beautiful lips. The emotions coursing through him were foreign, almost alarming. He'd somehow drifted into completely uncharted territory. Before he was ready, Tiff pulled away and with one last quick kiss on his cheek, turned and took her seat in the car.

The slamming of the door shut acted as an alarm clock for the Dom, jarring him awake. It was almost too late. As the car started to roll forward, he quickly knocked on her driver's side window. Tiff put the car in park and rolled down her window.

Lukus leaned down, placing his elbows on the window jam, leaning in closer. They spent a few long seconds looking into each other's eyes before Lukus found his words.

"Fuck slow. I'll be at your house tonight at six with a pizza and a bottle of wine. Meet me at the door in sexy lingerie and nothing else. Can you do that, baby?"

Tiffany's face lit up like Florida sunshine. She took her time, making him suffer before quietly responding with a simple, "Yes, Sir. I think I can."

With a flirty wink, she managed to roll up the window and Lukus watched as his best friend and his properly punished wife led the way down the alley with Tiffany driving behind them. He stayed glued to his spot until they turned and drove out of sight. Only then did Lukus see Derek leaning against the door, watching him carefully, a hard-to-read expression on his face.

"I don't even want to hear it."

"What? I wasn't gonna say a word."

"Like hell. You can't wait to give me shit."

"Why would I do that? You forget. I know you better than almost anyone else and I've told you before. You haven't been truly happy in years. That little girl who just drove away has lit your fire again. She's gonna give you a run for your money and I couldn't be happier for you, man."

Lukus detected the truth in his friend's words. "Be careful. She's no little girl."

"Yeah, I guess that's the truth. Markus told me

you guys woke him up at some point last night. Sounds like she's all woman."

"Hell, yeah."

"You know what this means, don't you?" Derek prodded him, pushing upright from the door.

"I'm afraid to even ask."

"It means we need to have some serious discussion about what's gonna happen around here. I'm pretty sure that little spitfire isn't gonna take kindly to you playing with and punishing subs on stage under the guise you're just doing your job."

Lukus had already been thinking the same thing. "She'll come around. I'm in charge."

"Ha! Not with that one, you aren't. At least not yet. Are you prepared to pack it in and close the club, because it just may come down to that with her?"

He rejected the idea of closing immediately. Lukus felt like he should have been upset at the thought of his life changing so drastically, so quickly, but he wasn't. He was excited. "Yeah, I've already started thinking about it. I'm sure I'll figure it all out. We'll have to see how things play out."

Derek seemed mildly surprised. "Holy shit, you're seriously considering you might need to retire at least from the front of the house activities? Shit, I thought she was gonna have to have a few meltdowns before you'd give in that easy. She must really be something special."

He had no doubt he would have some hard

decisions coming up if he decided to continue seeing Tiffany.

Who the hell am I kidding? There is no "if." I am going to keep seeing Tiff.

"She really is special," Lukus finally answered softly.

"So that's it. Just like that? Why don't you give it a bit more time to play out?"

"I don't need to. I know what I want and Tiffany is gonna give it to me."

"And what, pray tell, is that?"

Lukus broke out into a shit-eating grin. "I want it all. The whole thing. What you, James, and Markus already have."

"Holy fuck."

"Holy fuck is right."

Lukus turned to go back in and try to get some work done, doing his best to shout down the small voice warning him that he may end up losing the club if he stayed on the new course he'd just weaved on to.

CHAPTER TEN

MARKUS

"Markus, so good to see you. How long's it been?"

Markus found himself in a death-grip handshake with an old Northwestern law professor turned New York state senator. "Professor Withers. This is a surprise. I had no idea I'd run into you tonight. It has to be at least, what... eight, no, nine years? Damn, time flies!"

"Please, just Jonathan now. You aren't kidding about time flying. What brings you to this neck of the woods? I thought you were practicing in Chicago?" The senator released his grip long enough to deposit his empty champagne glass on the tray of a passing waiter, before grabbing two full crystal flutes and handing one to Markus.

"Thanks. I'm still in Chicago. I'm out here in Manhattan this week working with a new client. I'm headed back home tomorrow."

"You still at Brown and Cassidy?" Jonathon asked.

"Yep. Going on seven years now."

"What, and you don't have your name on the door yet?"

Markus chuckled. "Nope, not yet. I'm working on it, though."

"From what I hear, you're doing more than working on it. I've heard some pretty tall tales about your winning track record in court. If even half of them are true, I'm impressed. I always knew you were going to go far. Ever think about turning to politics?"

"Oh, hell no..." Markus then realized who he was talking to, and rushed to add, "No offense, Professor, or should I say, Senator?"

Markus was relieved when he was greeted with a hearty laugh. "Oh, no offense taken. To be truthful, it isn't all I thought it was going to be either. Damn gridlock everywhere I go. The longer I stay in the state senate, the more I realize it's a damn miracle anything ever gets done in this country."

Markus was only half listening to his old professor as the conversation turned to topics he couldn't care less about. He was much more interested in keeping his eyes glued to the entryway of the massive American grand hall. In New York City to meet with a new client, a federal judge who found himself on the wrong side of the law, he'd had managed to snag two invitations to a charity gala being hosted at the New York Metropolitan Museum. Looking around the expansive foyer, he caught a glimpse of several A-list celebrities, yet they weren't who he was anxious to see either.

I should've detoured to the hotel to pick her up. We might have even had time for a quickie in the limo.

He might have been buried in client meetings all day, but the anticipation of burying himself deep in his wife was never far from his thoughts. As they'd recently celebrated their third anniversary, an outsider might think it a bit late to be acting like newlyweds. Yet considering they'd had a near marriage-ending event occur less than one week before, Markus and his bride had spent every spare minute of their trip to New York reconnecting. He was determined to use this time away to get their marriage back on firm footing. Remembering last night's passionate marathon romp had all the blood rushing from his head to his cock.

Down, boy. We still have a few hours before you get to come out to play.

The room filled as the open-bar cocktail hour moved into full swing. He was starting to worry something might have been wrong when he spotted her. The sight of his elegant wife, paused at the top step of the entry of the grand foyer, took his breath away. A hush fell over the party. At first, Markus thought he was just tuning out the noise of the almost three hundred people in attendance, but as he walked towards her, he caught sight of several men who stopped mid-sentence to stare, mouths agape.

Dream on, boys. You can look, but don't even think of touching. She's all mine.

Brianna was wearing a slinky, plum dress that by all rights wasn't risqué on its own. The deep V-cut bodice was low enough to display the curves of her ample breasts, but the floor-length gown was classy. It was how the glimmering material hugged her sexy curves that left very little to the imagination as to what lay beneath. Her long, dark hair was pulled into a seductive updo, a few stray tendrils framed her radiant face. He knew the moment her scanning eyes found him. Her radiant smile aimed directly at him threatened to knock him on his ass.

They took a few seconds, undressing each other with their eyes across the room before his hot wife descended the marble steps, each step forward revealing her tanned legs through the thigh-high slit of her gown. Her eyes never left her husband's. Her sashay had the allure of a runway model. Even his companion, who'd been babbling along about the financial state of the country, was silenced mid-sentence, his attention riveted to the mysterious woman walking towards them.

As Brianna closed the distance between them, Markus observed the well-spoken Senator deteriorating into a bumbling teenager. By the time she stopped in front of them, Jonathan openly stared, his mouth agape.

Markus and Brianna spend time drinking each other in before he closed the remaining distance, taking her in his arms and pulling her tight against his chest. Over her shoulder he saw several jealous onlookers eyeing him with death stares.

"I was starting to worry about you, sweetheart. Is everything okay?" His intimate whisper against her ear triggered a shiver through her body.

Brianna threw her arms around his neck, nuzzling in close to whisper back. "I'm sorry Sir, but it took extra time before I got dressed to prepare myself as you requested."

Markus needed to see her eyes. He pulled back to gaze down upon his wife. "Does that mean you completed your full list, young lady?"

There was plenty of early evening light streaming in through the massive skylights. More than enough for Markus to catch the adorable blush highlighting his wife's cheeks. With a surge of joy, he remembered she was so much more than just his wife now. All week long he kept getting reminded of their previous weekend. The weekend when everything had changed between them. Sitting in client meetings, on conference calls, awakened in the middle of the night in a cold sweat, or even now, standing in the middle of the crowded Metropolitan Museum, the memories resurfaced of how close he had come to losing the love of his life. He reacted instinctively by hugging her closer, if that was possible, subconsciously daring her to try to get away.

Brianna was finally able to answer. "Yes, Sir."

"Very good. Of course, I'll have to do my own personal inspection. In fact, I have a few other preparations you're gonna need to make now that you're here." He flashed her a mischievous smile before continuing. "But, you're safe for now. Come, my dear. There's someone I'd like you to meet."

Releasing her reluctantly, Markus instead reached for her hand, turning back to his old professor, who was still standing there with the same silly look on his face. "Professor, or should I say Senator Withers, I'd like to introduce you to my wife, Brianna. Sweetheart, I bumped into an old professor from Northwestern while I was waiting for you to join me. Professor Withers retired from the life of academia and is now a New York state senator."

To his credit, the senator recovered his composure and captured Brianna's other hand, bringing it to his lips to gallantly place a light kiss. "It's an absolute pleasure to meet you, Brianna." He glanced sideways at the younger lawyer. "Damn, Markus. Some guys have all the luck."

Before Markus could reply, Brianna surprised

both men with her quick retort. "Oh, but Senator, you have it all wrong. I'm the lucky one in this relationship." Her chocolate brown eyes turned back to her husband, shining with an adorable mix of love and lust.

Jonathan chuckled as he released her hand in time to nab another flute of champagne to offer to Brianna. "Well, I can see you've married well, Mr. Lambert." Raising his glass, he continued. "I'd like to offer a salute to your beautiful wife here, that is if you'll stop undressing her with your eyes long enough to toast."

It took several long seconds for his words to register before Markus reluctantly tore his gaze away from his wife to smile at his old professor. "Looks like I've been caught red-handed. I'll have to settle for a toast." As he winked at Brianna, he couldn't stop the playful grin from emerging.

If only Jonathan knew how close I am to doing exactly as I promised. If we were at The Punishment Pit instead of The Met, I'd be balls-deep already.

"To the newlyweds. I can always spot a couple who haven't quite finished their honeymoon yet. How many months have you been married?"

Markus let Brianna take the question. "Actually, we just celebrated our third anniversary."

"Well, that explains it. At three months, I'd still be bringing her along on my business trips, too."

"No, sir. You misunderstood. We just

celebrated our third *year* of marriage. I'm just lucky he still likes me to tag along. I hate when he's gone overnight for work."

The professor glanced back at Markus, as if to validate her claim. "Well I'll be damned. Now I'm really jealous. I don't think my ex-wife looked at me like that on our wedding night, let alone three years in."

Moving next to Bri, Markus slipped his arm intimately around her waist, pulling her close. Raising his glass, he offered up a toast. "To my beautiful wife. I love you more every single day, baby."

They all took time to sip the expensive bubbly before Markus moved in, capturing her lips in a modest kiss.

From inside Brianna's clutch, the muffled sound of her cell phone ringing interrupted them.

Damn that woman. It's like she knows the second we are kissing.

Brianna looked guilty as she pulled out of their embrace to pick up the call before it rolled over to voicemail. Just before she pressed *answer*, she had the nerve to play innocent. "What?"

"Don't *what* me, young lady. That's the third kiss this week she's interrupted."

Brianna wasn't playing fair as she flashed her most playful grin his way. "She's just nervous, honey. She needs lots of advice. Can I take it? Pretty please?"

Little did she know... he couldn't say no to her if he'd tried. They might have spent much of the week laying the groundwork of the new power exchange dynamics in their marriage, but as the week had progressed, Markus had had to acknowledge that while he may officially be his wife's Dominant, she still had the ability to bring him to his knees with a simple smile, the scent of her arousal, a light touch of her hand. This week he'd been more aware than ever of the delicate dance of a D/s relationship.

To her credit, Bri waited obediently. At his simple nod, she grinned victoriously as she pressed *answer* just in time. "Tiff, you there?"

Markus should have been mad at the intrusion of the call, but he loved his wife's best friend too much to be angry. Besides, she was most likely calling for more advice on how to handle her budding D/s relationship with his own best friend. Markus felt a bit guilty about hiding the fact from his wife that Lukus had called him twice this week for advice.

Interrupting her call, Markus leaned close. "I'm going to grab us some appetizers from the buffet. I'll be back in a couple minutes and we'll find our table. Wrap it up before I get back."

Markus delivered a quick kiss and, on a whim, brushed her ass just long enough to send the signal loud and clear to the men standing nearby to keep their mitts off his woman.

Tearing himself away, he turned to his old professor. "Come on, Jonathan. I'll buy you an appetizer."

"So nice of you, cheap bastard, considering they're complimentary."

Brianna

"Brianna, are you there?" Tiffany asked.

"Yeah. Sorry about that. I was a little distracted."

"Oh, no. I didn't interrupt you guys having sex again, did I?"

Brianna giggled. "No, not this time. We're actually out at a fundraiser. I only have a few minutes before Markus gets back. What's up? Everything okay at the shop?"

A wave of guilt swept over Brianna as she remembered that she had left her best friend and second in command behind in Chicago to hold down the fort all week at The Beauty Box. She should have been there, taking care of business, so her best friend could focus on her new relationship with her yummy new boyfriend.

"Yeah, yeah. Everything is fine, although a bit

slow at the shop. It rained most of the day. We didn't have any walk-ins. That's not why I'm calling."

"Okay. So, I assume this call has something to do with the really hot guy with tight abs, sexy five o'clock shadow, and dreamy green eyes who has a nasty habit of threatening to spank you every night."

"You know, that's what has me freaked out. He's driven out to my place three nights in a row this week and honestly, he's been an absolute gentleman, assuming a gentleman is allowed to make love until he makes his woman scream." Tiffany giggled self-consciously before spitting out what had her worried. "Anyway, tonight is going to be different. It's the first time I'm going down to his loft and Bri, I'm coming unhinged. I've loved every minute of our time together this week. We've spent hours talking, getting to know each other, and it's freaking me out. I keep waiting to find out something about him that is going to burst the bubble, but it just hasn't happened. It's terrible."

Bri 'couldn't help but laugh at her friend. "Oh, I agree. It sounds absolutely horrible. I can see why you're upset."

"Stop laughing at me. You know what I mean."

"No, Tiff. I don't. Do you even hear yourself? You like him. He likes you. The word *terrible* doesn't belong in this conversation."

"Well, it will belong if I end up getting my heart broken. I really like him, Bri. This week has been like a dream so far, but I'm scared."

"Of what?"

"Him," Tiff said.

"Not good enough. Of what, really?"

"I don't know. I guess, by his own admission, he doesn't do relationships. I can't stop myself from thinking about what the shelf life is for a relationship like ours."

"Stop. Right now. You do this all the time. Stop thinking. Stop worrying."

"But tonight is the first night I'll be at the club when it's open. What if I do something wrong? What if I embarrass him? What if he asks me to do things I don't want to do? What if—"

Bri interrupted her. "Stop!" The telltale signs of her best friend's panic were evident in the heavy breathing at the other end of the line. "Tiff, you need to take a deep breath and calm down. There is no way you're going to do something embarrassing, and truly, haven't you figured out by now that Lukus will never make you do anything you don't feel comfortable doing? You have your safeword, right?"

"Yes, but I'm not sure I can use it."

"Of course you can, if you need to."

"I just don't want to disappoint him. He keeps making a big deal about how different I am from any other woman he has spent time with, and since the women he hangs out with are sex slaves or submissives, that translates to me being a wimpy, vanilla sex bore who he is going to toss aside within the month. I mean seriously, how am I going to satisfy him when he has naked women throwing themselves at him all day long? I've been fooling myself all week thinking he is a normal guy, but who the hell am I kidding? He owns a sex club. He is the Master's Master. He makes a living off punishing naughty submissives. How long do you think he's going to be satisfied playing house with me out in the suburbs?"

"That's enough. We went through this yesterday. I'll go through it again now and tomorrow, and the next day, until you get it through your head. Stop trying to sabotage this before you even hit your one-week mark. Yes, he owns a sex club; a sex club he hasn't been spending time at since he met you. And it's not his whole life. He also owns a very successful security firm. Let me ask you. Has Lukus done anything to you this week to make you think he is going to try to force you into a twenty-four seven D/s relationship?"

"No."

Bri continued. "Has he acted like Master Lukus, or just plain Lukus?"

"Mostly just Lukus. Let's face it. He can't just turn off that sexy *I'm-in-charge-here* attitude."

"Well, thank goodness for that. It really is yummy, isn't it? But I digress. Has he made crazy promises to you just trying to get in your pants?"

"No, but in all fairness, he didn't need to. He got in my pants without any promises."

Brianna chuckled. "Yeah, right. Well, regardless, has he lied to you?"

"No."

"Treated you like shit or hurt you?"

"No."

"And, what *did* he do for you this week? Did he take you out to dinner?"

"Yes, every night. He said he didn't want to make me cook after working all day," Tiff admitted.

"Oh, what an ogre. Did he act like Master Lukus, forcing you to be naked and kneeling at his feet when you got back to your place?"

That got a giggle out of her best friend. "No to the kneeling part, but we have been naked for a fair amount of our time together."

"Seriously, Tiff. Are you hearing yourself? This guy is one in a million. Stop trying to scare yourself into screwing it up."

Almost thirty seconds of silence passed; Brianna became worried that the call had dropped when she finally heard her best friend's sigh. "You're right. I just need to stay calm. He keeps telling me that we just need to take it one day at a time."

"Smart man."

Brianna was startled by strong arms wrapping around her waist from behind her. She could feel the athletic body of her husband as he pulled her tight against his chest. "Why, thank you. I hear you ladies are talking about me."

Brianna rested her head back on his shoulder, still holding the phone to her ear. "Yes, honey. We were just saying what a smart man you are."

"Liar. You know what the penalty is for lying to me, don't you?" His whisper was delivered as he brushed her ear lobe with his lips.

Brianna's heart rate ratcheted up a notch. He pulled her tighter as a shiver raced through her at the thought of being turned over his lap for a bare-bottomed spanking. She was tempted to lay another fib on him, just to get her *reward*. For most women, the promise of a spanking would be a punishment, but to her, the intimacy of a spanking —coupled with her unusually high pain tolerance— translated to a reward.

"Yes, sir."

"Are you ladies just about wrapped up on your call? I have Jonathan saving us seats. They're filling up fast. Say your goodbyes."

"But Markus, she needs some moral support. She's on her way to the club."

Markus released his wife to reach for her cell phone. "Let me talk with her."

"I don't know if that's such a great idea."

"Bri, hand me the phone, please."

"Okay, but be nice." He was nice enough to put the call on speaker so Bri could continue to hear it.

Markus questioned her friend. "Tiff, are you in the car?"

"Yes. I'm headed down to see Lukus. He couldn't get away tonight."

"Okay. Please tell me you are using your Bluetooth headset." Dead silence on the other end of the phone. "Tiffany?"

When the silence dragged on, Markus pressed her. "Are you or are you not following the law of Illinois and using a hands-free device to talk on the phone while driving?"

"Dammit, he told you, didn't he?"

Markus chuckled. "Well, are you? And I'd think twice about lying, young lady."

"Grrr. I can't believe this. You're going to tell him, aren't you?"

"No. I won't need to, because you're going to tell him. Right away. Tonight."

"But, Markus, no. You don't understand."

"I understand perfectly. Less than twenty-four hours ago you got a ticket for speeding in a construction zone while talking on your cell phone. It's going to cost you a pretty penny in fines. Lukus asked you to go out and buy a Bluetooth last night. Why aren't you using it?" Markus asked.

"I forgot to charge it. Markus, please. I promise

I'll use it tomorrow, but I can't tell him. He'll... well, he will—"

"He'll spank your ass."

The sound of a screaming Tiffany could be heard over Bri's husband's chuckle. Several people standing nearby stopped their conversation to look their way. Bri blushed self-consciously, but Markus was oblivious to their growing audience. He seemed to be enjoying himself entirely too much. Brianna had to remind herself that her best friend hadn't exactly gotten used to the idea of dating a guy who wouldn't hesitate to spank her.

"I can't believe this. How did you know?" Tiff said eventually.

"Well, I have a secret for you. Lukus has been calling me for advice as often as you have been calling my wife. So, let me give you some advice. I'll tell you what I told him. Stop trying to analyze this to death. He likes you, a lot. You like him, a lot. You may come from different backgrounds, but not as different as you may think. I am in a unique position of knowing you both very well, so I'm telling you to trust him."

"But, what if I get my heart trampled on?"

"And, what if you don't? What if you walk away and never know? Now, it's time you stop talking on your phone and focus on driving. Got that?"

"Yes, *Sir*." Tiffany's signature sass was coming through loud and clear with her short answer.

"I'd be careful. That attitude is going to get you into trouble."

"Oh believe me, it already has. Several times."

Markus chuckled. "Yes, I heard all about that, too. For what it's worth, Lukus feels as off-base as you do."

"Really?"

Bri heard hope in her best friend's voice.

"Really. I've known Lukus for going on fourteen years now, and I've never seen him like this."

"Thanks, Markus. I feel so much better now after talking with you and Bri."

"You're welcome, Tiff. Now, seriously. Stop calling my wife. You will see her tomorrow afternoon, and I'm planning on keeping her very busy between now and then."

Brianna caught the look of longing in her husband's eyes as they locked their gaze. The room began to feel warm from the lustful look on his face.

"Hello, you guys still there?" Tiffany's voice brought them back to the moment.

"I'll talk to you tomorrow, Tiff. Just try to have fun tonight, okay?" Brianna said.

"Okay, you guys too. I'll talk to you tomorrow."

The call cut off before Brianna could say goodbye. She smiled up at her husband. "So, Lukus has been calling you?"

"Yep."

"And..."

"And, nothing. Let's go eat," he said.

"You aren't going to tell me any more about what you guys talked about, are you?"

"Nope. Let's go eat so we can leave. I suddenly have a desire for us to be alone."

CHAPTER ELEVEN

TIFFANY

Tiffany pushed *end* on the call. She was so lost in thought as she reached over to the passenger seat to throw her phone in her purse, she almost missed the fact that traffic had stopped dead in the middle of the busy expressway ahead. She focused on the road just in time to slam on her brakes, projecting the entire contents of her open purse onto the floor.

"Fuck!" At the sound of her own expletive, she broke out into a nervous laugh before talking out loud to the empty car. "That's it, Tiff. It's not bad enough Lukus is going to be pissed you aren't wearing the new Bluetooth, but now you're going to crash your car and get caught cussing. Maybe you should just turn around and head home now while you can still sit down."

Several minutes later, traffic started inching

forward again, and she could just make out the emergency vehicle's lights up ahead.

Just great. Now I can add being late to the list of punishable offenses.

If she was honest with herself, she wasn't afraid of Lukus, in spite of what she might have led Markus to believe. Not really. Sure, Lukus had been dominant with her at times this week, but truly, she'd loved every single minute of their time together, including... or more accurately, *especially*... the night he'd demonstrated the many joys of an erotic spanking.

The man is a freaking sex god. I'm pretty sure I've had more orgasms courtesy of Lukus Mitchell in one week than by all my other boyfriends combined.

No, it was not the sex or even the threat of a spanking that had Tiffany on edge tonight. She wasn't sure what was at the heart of her unease. What she did know was that tension had been building within her with each glorious day spent with Lukus since meeting him last weekend.

She was still surprised he'd spent almost every night at her townhouse in the suburbs. That he drove to her three evenings in a row was amazing enough, but she couldn't believe he'd slept over, choosing to get up early to drive back to the city in rush-hour traffic, rather than miss snuggling her all night long. She had never slept better—or worse— than this week. Unfortunately, the return of Tiff's

Jake nightmares was a side-effect of being in her first BDSM relationship.

Damn, I wish Bri and I had never met Jake Davenport.

So far, her dreams of Jake hurting her and threatening her family was the only negative outcome of meeting Lukus. It annoyed her in her waking hours because the two men couldn't have been more different from each other if they'd tried. Regardless, her re-exposure to the BDSM lifestyle had thrown her back into nightmares she'd thought were long gone. Remembering how gentle and reassuring Lukus had been as he comforted her when she was hit with a bad dream still surprised her. She'd expected him to lose his patience with her by now, but it hadn't happened.

Even last night, when they had taken their first break from each other, they ended up talking on the phone for an hour, talking about everything and nothing at the same time. After hanging up, she had sat with a glass of wine, thinking through all she'd learned about his childhood; his family, his friends, his businesses—he talked freely about them all. She'd been waiting for some big bombshell to blow up in her face, like finding out he had a wife stashed away somewhere. Instead, he kept proving to her how truly amazing he and she really were.

In her mind, Tiff knew Brianna was right; she should just enjoy the ride, but her anxious mind was driving her emotions right now. She couldn't shake the feeling that her heart had left the comfortably safe road and was now forging a new path she had never treaded before. She wasn't sure if knowing Lukus had never been this far off the road emotionally made her feel better or worse. They clearly had a deep connection. The question was—how long would it last, and how would she survive when it ended?

Tiff's worrying was interrupted by her phone ringing from the passenger side floor. It was his ring tone.

Just great. I'm screwed. I can't answer because I don't have my Bluetooth. I can't reach it anyway.

According to her dashboard clock, she was already ten minutes late. Luckily, she was past the accident and already exiting the expressway. She took the time to pull into a gas station to park and retrieve her phone to make a quick call. He answered on the first ring.

"You're late."

That was so Lukus. "Well, hello to you, too. There's an accident on the Eisenhower. I'm past it now. I should be there in about ten minutes."

"Great. I'm starving. I cooked. I think you're going to like it."

"So you don't want me to cook after a long day of working, but you get to cook?"

"Yep. I make the rules, remember?" he said.

"Hmmm. I don't recall agreeing to that."

"Oh, I'm sure you meant to. It's front and

center in that contract I've been trying to get you to read through. The rules are outlined... right before agreeing to let me spank that beautiful ass of yours when you break one of them." His deep chuckle reassured her, yet the mention of the contract threw her into a whole new level of anxiety.

She was lost in thought for long enough that Lukus had to make sure she was still there. "Hey, did I lose you?"

"No, I'm here."

"You're thinking again, aren't you?" he asked.

"I have a brain. I tend to think from time to time, yes."

"Sass. You are so full of sass, Miss O'Sullivan. Talk."

Tiffany hated that even over the phone he could read her like a book. "It's nothing."

"One."

"You know I hate you counting."

"You know I hate you hiding things from me."

He patiently waited thirty long seconds, knowing she would eventually cave. She always did. "You mentioned the contract again. I told you Lukus, I don't want a contract between us."

"And I told you, baby, it's not meant to be some binding document. It is just gonna help me understand where your head is at on a few things, that's all."

"And I told you, honey, that we don't need a

piece of paper to do that. Just ask me. Talk to me," she replied.

"This isn't the time or the place for this conversation. I need to see your eyes. You can't hide anything from me when I can see your eyes."

An unladylike snort erupted from Tiffany. "Believe me, you don't need to see my eyes. Sometimes I think you have secret cameras watching me. It is spooky how you can read me even over the phone."

"Hey, not a bad idea. Okay, you should almost be here by now. I'll let Derek know. He's gonna meet you at the entrance and will park your car for you. I don't want you walking in the alley alone after dark," Lukus said.

"It's barely dark. I'm sure I'll be fine."

"Must you argue with me at every turn? Can't you at least let me pretend I might have a chance at controlling this relationship like the Dom that I am?"

Tiff wanted to be angry, but as always when he got bossy, she knew he was only trying to protect her. It helped her answer without so much as a trace of annoyance. "I'm sorry. I'll be happy to let Derek park my car."

"Thank you. Was that so hard?"

"I guess not."

"Great. You here yet?" he asked.

Oh, no.

"Um, not quite yet. I'll be there in like ten minutes."

"You said that ten minutes ago."

"Well, since I'm not moving, that's still the plan."

Silence greeted her until he proved once again he had secret cameras watching her. "You didn't use your new Bluetooth, did you?" he said eventually.

"Damn. How do you do that? No, I didn't charge it, okay? I'm sorry. But I did pull over to use my phone instead of calling you while I was driving. That has to count for something."

"We'll talk about this when I see you."

"Talk?"

"Talk."

"Okay."

"Derek is gonna give you the code for the alley door. Hang a hard left when you get in the door; that hall will take you to the back of house, and the elevator to my loft. I also programmed your code for all of the doors you'll need to pass through."

"But not the actual club." The annoyance in her tone was back.

"Tiff. We discussed this. You aren't ready for the club yet. Hell, I'm not ready to have you in the club yet."

"I don't understand. Bri and I used to go to BDSM clubs years ago. I'm not going to freak out."

"We'll talk when you get here. Hang up and drive," he said.

"So bossy."

"So sassy."

"Bye."

"Bye, baby."

Tiff threw the phone in her purse and drove off, thinking about the possible reasons behind his refusal to let her see the main floor of The Punishment Pit. She'd been in the club while it was closed last Saturday night, so it couldn't be the club itself. That meant it had to be what happened there when it was open. The closer she got, the more curious she got. By the time she was pulling up at the nondescript entrance, marked only with *TPP 7969* on the cold steel door, her curiosity had turned into an insatiable need to know. The thought of being a voyeur at the punishment club had her panties turning damp.

Derek burst out of the door, looking every bit the hulking body builder she remembered from the weekend before. Had she met him in this alley under different circumstances, he would have scared the shit out of her. Instead, he reached in to help her from her car and promptly scooped her up into a tight bear hug that had her high heels leaving the pavement. She felt like a rag doll.

"Tiffany! Thank God you're here. He's driving me nuts today." After he finally put her back on her feet, she pulled back enough to look up at his lopsided smile and dark brown eyes. "Promise me you'll move in, tonight," Derek continued. "He missed seeing you for one night, and was driving me and the security crew fucking crazy all day."

"Hi to you, too, Derek. And the last time I checked, Lukus never asked me to move in. Considering we've known each other for exactly five days, that seems a bit ridiculous."

"Fuck. Well, don't take too long. His mood swings are gonna kill us. One minute he is all happy and relaxed, and the next he is biting someone's head off."

"And what makes you think his mood swings have anything to do with me? Maybe he's coming down with something?" she said.

"Oh, he's coming down with something all right. It's called Tiffany O'Sullivan."

Tiff managed a nervous snicker. "I think you're exaggerating, but still, thanks Derek. Lukus talks about you a lot. I know you're important to him."

"Just trust him." Derek smiled at her. He reached into the pocket of his tight jeans to pull out a keycard, along with a post-it note containing a six-digit code. "Here's your keycard and your entrance code. It'll get you into the back of house as well as Lukus's office and the elevator. Insert the card, then push the seventh floor to get to the loft."

Tiffany collected her overnight bag, taking a minute to throw all the contents of her purse from the floor back into her bag, before closing the car door. Derek zoomed off in her car as she turned to the door. She forced herself to take a calming breath before punching in her entry code.

The pounding music from the club greeted her as she stepped into the dim hall. The hallway opened up to the grand foyer that led to the main club entrance. She paused a moment, remembering the last time she'd been here, being led by Lukus. He had stood before that final door, giving her a last chance to turn around and leave.

Thank God I stayed.

In that moment she was sure she had done the right thing by staying; and that simple truth calmed her. She was about to turn left when the club door burst open. Two men dressed in suits, their ties loosened at the neck, strode out. They looked like businessmen who had stopped by for a drink on their way home from the office.

Tiff's curiosity had her calling out to them. "Can you hold the door, please?"

The men looked up. Tiff had to fight the urge to laugh at their reaction to seeing her there. She should have known the second their eyes started undressing her that she'd made a mistake, but in for a penny, in for a pound. She rushed forward, brushing between them to sprint through the door before they could stop her. "Thanks, boys." For a second, she was afraid they were going to follow her back into the club. She was relieved when the door slammed shut behind her, trapping her on the main floor of The Punishment Pit.

Like last time, dance music was playing just loud enough to lend a nightclub feel to the space. Unlike last time, she was not alone. It was still early by sex club standards... something she was grateful for. She stood planted near the door, taking in the sight of the dozen or so couples sprinkled throughout the space. Some were sitting in comfortable couches and lounge chairs, others milling about near the lengthy bar to the left. The two-story red velvet curtains shielded the front of the stage, hiding the dungeon behind. She shivered, remembering the sight of Lukus in action on that stage with Markus as they had punished Brianna the night she'd met him.

She was barraged by conflicting emotions. It had been both exciting and horrific being forced to watch, unable to help her best friend. Yet, even she had to acknowledge Brianna deserved everything her husband and his best friend had dished out, considering she'd cheated on him with that asshole, Jake, the day before. It truly was a miracle how everything had worked out, not only for Brianna and Markus, but for her and Lukus as well.

The heavy beat of the music lent a dance club feel to the space, but as Tiffany's eyes adjusted to the dim lighting of the pre-show club, the sights that greeted her reminded her she was definitely in a sex club. Scratch that. Not just any sex club, but a

BDSM sex club. There was absolutely no doubt about it.

The only woman—besides herself, of course—who was wearing clothes, happened to be in a full-body latex suit, facemask included. As if being encased in a skin-tight, body-hugging suit wouldn't be uncomfortable enough, her Dom had been nice enough to prop per mouth wide open with a large, metal spreader gag.

At least she isn't going to suffocate.

The only body part showing other than her gag-opened lips were her clamp-covered lower lips. Courtesy of her spread legs, Tiff could see heavy gage clamps biting into both sides of her enlarged labia. Bulky weights hung from the metal, ensuring the delivery of constant burning pain. Her arms stretched high above her head, held secure by manacles hanging from the many rafters over the audience pit.

Tiff allowed herself a few minutes to inspect the rest of the space, and found multiple nooks of torture available for club members to enjoy. It was as if every piece of furniture doubled as a punishment device or restraint. While some Doms relaxed with drinks, their submissives kneeling obediently nearby as they shot the shit after a long day at the office, others made use of the plethora of punishment devices on hand. The heat in Tiffany's core percolated at the sight of a naughty sub thrown over the back of a couch, her Master lighting up her ass with his thick belt.

She watched curiously as several waitresses mingled through the club. While they may have taken drink or food orders like normal servers, to work at The Punishment Pit, they clearly had to possess other important attributes. For one thing, they all appeared to boast double D sized breasts, showcased by the skimpy, form-fitting corsets doubling as a uniform. While their waists were cinched painfully tight, forcing their bodies into an hourglass shape, the cup-less bodice of the uniform was cut in a way to provide a shelf, prominently promoting their bare busts. The waitress nearest Tiff sported not only heavy nipple piercings, but welts of a recent caning also marked her ample breasts.

Soon, a second waitress passed by, close enough for Tiffany to make out the contents of her small bar tray. Mingled with one martini glass and a bottle of imported beer was a curious collection of sexual aids, being passed out like free swag items at a party. Tiff made out several packets of condoms, a pair of nipple clamps, a small bottle of lube, a sturdy hairbrush, and most surprising, several feathers.

The sound of a text dinging on her cell phone reminded her she was not where she was supposed to be. She'd planned to only take a quick peek at the club, but she'd lingered long enough that Lukus was probably looking for her.

I need to get the hell out of here, and quick.

As she spun to leave the same way she had come in, the door flung open and two couples barged forward, almost knocking her over. The men were a bit older, and much heavier than the other members in attendance. She stifled a snicker after deciding they looked more like nerdy accountants than Doms. Regardless, the two scantily clad women following closely behind, tethered to them by their collar and leash, confirmed that the men were indeed Doms. They stopped short in front of Tiff, too close for comfort.

"Excuse me, gentlemen. I was just leaving."

"Oh damn, don't tell me we're too late to buy you a drink, little lady. I think you need to stay long enough for us to get to know you better."

Tiffany observed the predatory glare in the men's eyes. They didn't even try to hide that they were checking out every inch of her body. She regretted wearing a low-cut blouse and short skirt. Both had been chosen specifically to entice Lukus into ravishing her, not to attract the attention of these unsavory characters. She tried brushing past them, but they were bold enough to block her way, disgustingly laying their hands on her. She was furious.

"Let me go, this instant."

"Listen, you know the rules. Are you a

Domme?" Before she could think fast enough to reply, he laughed. "Of course you aren't. If you're a Domme, I'm Mickey Mouse. And since I don't see a collar, not even a house collar, you're fair game, little lady. Now, come have a drink with us."

Quickly swinging her around, the men each took one of her arms and started forcibly shuffling her towards the bar. Tiff tried digging in her heels to stop their forward movement, but it wasn't working. "You guys are making a really big mistake. You need to let me go, right now. I need to leave."

"Oh come on, just one drink while we get to know you a bit better. Who knows? Maybe you'll decide you'd like to stay and play with us. My brother and I can show you a good time tonight."

Their grip cut into her arms; she worried they might leave a mark Lukus was going to see. She knew she needed to get out of here and up to the loft before he came looking for her. With a quick yank, she finally pulled free, only to fall backwards against a muscular chest that felt suspiciously like Lukus. Conflicting emotions invaded. She was happy he was there to help her deal with these two yahoos, but she knew she was in big trouble for coming into the club alone. She hit a whole new level of fear when the man holding her tightly against him spoke.

"What do we have here? Fresh meat?"

Shit. It's not Lukus.

She was grateful when she felt his grip

loosening. Her brief moment of relief was short-lived. As he twirled her around to face him, she came face to face with the most menacing looking man she had ever had the displeasure to meet in her twenty-seven years. A shiver consumed her as his predatory eyes drank her in as if she was property to be used as desired. When his eyes returned to hers, she knew she was in big trouble.

You really got yourself into a hot mess this time, Tiff. Lukus is going to wail on your ass when he finds you.

As his grip on her tightened, she struggled to wrench free. "Um, excuse me. Let me go. I'm not in the right place. I need to leave."

Things went from bad to worse when the unwelcome Dom grabbed her long hair and yanked it hard, forcing her neck to snap back so she was forced to stare straight into his pockmark-filled face. He wasn't much taller than she was, which provided her with the displeasure of looking him straight in the eye as she felt his other hand cupping her ass, pulling her tight against him. "But you just got here. I see you're unattached. A beautiful woman like you shouldn't be in a place like this alone. I'll protect you."

Acting braver than she felt, she retorted, "And who the hell is going to protect me from you?" Without thinking, the sassy response was out. The predatory look in his eyes turned to fury.

"You little bitch. Someone needs to teach you some manners."

Way to go Tiff. I hope I'm alive long enough for Lukus to save me.

To be continued in book four of the Punishment Pit series, *Balancing it All*. Preorder/buy it now! Check out this short excerpt.

Excerpt from *Balancing it All~ Book Four*

Lukus

Lukus was throwing the bread sticks into the oven to warm up when the cell phone in his pocket vibrated. He decided to let it roll to voicemail. There was only one person he wanted to talk to right now, and she was in the elevator on her way up to the loft.

I wonder if we'll have time for a quickie before we eat.

They'd been damn near inseparable since meeting the weekend before, and yesterday his intense attraction to Tiffany had started to scare him after he'd realized he couldn't make it through an hour without thinking about her. Scratch that. He couldn't make it an hour without obsessing about her. He was a Dom; in control of anything and everything in his life. It had pissed him off that he couldn't just turn off the need to see her—touch her—talk to her—fuck her.

As if he'd needed to prove he was stronger than her magnetic pull, he'd forced himself to stay away from her last night. His brain knew they needed the break from each other to catch their breath. It was at around 11 p.m., when he'd found himself in the elevator with car keys in hand to drive out to her place in the burbs, that the depth of his problem had hit him hard.

He'd managed to turn himself around and return to his loft, but he'd slept like shit, worried about her needing his comfort when the nightmares of that asshole, Jake, woke her. By 4 a.m. he had given up on sleep, deciding to get an early start on his day rather than lie in bed feeling like a fucking lovesick puppy.

Lukus's phone vibrated again. "Dammit." It was clear someone wanted to talk to him, and now. "This better be good."

It had been his club manager, Ethan, calling. "We have a problem."

"Funny. That's why I hired you. To take care of the problems."

"I think you're gonna want to handle this one yourself."

"I doubt it. Find Derek. He should be back soon from parking Tiff's car."

"I don't think this can wait," Ethan said.

"Is the place on fire? If not, it can wait."

"Robinson is here."

"Fuck. Well, it was bound to happen at some point. His suspension is up. He's cleared to return to the club."

"That's not the only problem."

Lukus opened the oven to check on the lasagna and bread sticks. Deciding to leave them in for a minute longer, he continued, "Spit it out, will ya? This cryptic shit is driving me nuts."

"Did your girlfriend make it up there yet?"

The first alarm bell went off. "No. She should..." It hit him that there'd been plenty of time for Tiffany to have made it up to the loft. "Fuck."

"Yep. I'm not sure how she got in, but I came out front from the storage closet with a case of Heineken, and saw a crowd gathering in front of the bar. I was surprised 'cause it's still early. It took me a minute to figure out what's going on, but there's a hot blonde surrounded by Robinson and the Bronson twins. She doesn't belong."

"Why do you think it's Tiffany?"

"For starters, she looks like a dead ringer of how Derek described her," Ethan said. "But mainly, because she's the only woman I've seen in the club fully dressed, looking like she just came from the office. She has no collar and she looks scared shitless."

"God dammit. I can't fucking believe it. I'm gonna wail on her ass so hard she isn't going to sit down for a week."

"Well, you'd better hurry. It seems like she just said something that totally pissed Robinson off. He looks like he's going to beat you to it."

Lukus was already sprinting to the stairwell, knowing it was faster than waiting for the elevator. "Over my dead body. Get out there and break it up. Protect her at all costs until I get there."

"You got it, boss." The call ended as both men moved into action.

Lukus's mind raced about all the bad things Robinson might do to his Tiff as he took the stairs two at a time, going as fast as he could without breaking his neck.

On some level he knew he couldn't pin the blame for this situation on Robinson, even if he was a top-notch asshole. He had so wanted to expel him from the club when Robinson, a sadistic bastard, put his sub-turned-slave in the hospital six weeks ago. If only the woman had pressed charges, Lukus could have expelled him, but she moved back in with him after her release from the hospital. Following the strict by-laws of the club contracts, the most Lukus could sanction him with was a one-month suspension from stepping foot on club property. That one month had ended last weekend.

He'd better not hurt a hair on her head or he's dead.

Lukus made it to the first floor in one piece and took the quickest route to the club floor by rushing across the stage and through the red velvet stage curtains. The room was dimly lit, but he could make out the crowd gathered in front of the bar, as Ethan described. He stopped long enough to assess the situation. His blood started to boil when he saw Robinson pulling Tiffany's hair and grabbing her ass.

I'm glad I have Markus on retainer. There's a good chance I might end up in jail tonight.

Preorder/buy it now!

USA Today Bestselling Author Livia Grant lives in Chicago with her husband and furry rescue dog named Max. She is fortunate to have been able to travel extensively and as much as she loves to visit places around the globe, the Midwest and its changing seasons will always be home. Livia's readers appreciate her riveting stories filled with deep, character driven plots, often spiced with elements of BDSM.

- Livia's Website: http://www. liviagrant.com/newsletter
- Join Livia's Facebook Group: The Passion Vault
- Facebook Author Page to Like: https:// www.facebook.com/pages/Livia-Grant/877459968945358
- Goodreads: https://www.goodreads. com/author/show/ 8474605.Livia_Grant
- BookBub: https://www.bookbub.com/ profile/livia-grant

ALSO BY LIVIA GRANT

Connect to Livia's books through her website here.

Black Light Series

Infamous Love, A Black Light Prequel

Black Light: Rocked

Black Light: Valentine Roulette

Black Light: Rescued

Black Light: Roulette Redux

Complicated Love

Black Light: Celebrity Roulette

Black Light: Purged

Black Light: Scandalized

Black Light: Roulette War

Black Light: The Beginning

Black Light: Rolled - coming November, 2020

Punishment Pit Series

Wanting it All

Securing it All

Having it All - Release 9/22/20

Balancing it All - Release 10/6/20

Defending it All - Release 10/27/20

Protecting it All - Release 11/17/20

Expecting it All - Release 12/1/20

Stand Alone Books

Blessed Betrayal

Royalty, American Style

Alpha's Capture (as Livia Bourne)

Blinding Salvation (as Livia Bourne)

Don't miss Livia's next book!

Sign-up for Livia's Newsletter

Follow Livia on BookBub

BLACK COLLAR PRESS

Black Collar Press is a small publishing house started by authors Livia Grant and Jennifer Bene in late 2016. The purpose was simple - to create a place where the erotic, kinky, and exciting worlds they love to explore could thrive and be joined by other like-minded authors.

If this is something that interests you, please go to the Black Collar Press website and read through the FAQs. If your questions are not answered there, please contact us directly at: blackcollarpress@gmail.com

Where to find Black Collar Press:

- Website: http://www. blackcollarpress.com/
- Facebook: https://www. facebook.com/blackcollarpress/

- Twitter: https://twitter.com/BlackCollarPres
- Black Light East and West may be fictitious, but you can now join our very real Facebook Group for Black Light Fans - Black Light Central

Made in the USA
Columbia, SC
08 February 2021